Anuradha Ayyar

Cover Illustration By:
Anjana Ayyar

INDIA · SINGAPORE · MALAYSIA

Copyright © Anuradha Ayyar 2023
All Rights Reserved.

ISBN 979-8-88869-958-4

This book has been published with all efforts taken to make the material error-free after the consent of the author. However, the author and the publisher do not assume and hereby disclaim any liability to any party for any loss, damage, or disruption caused by errors or omissions, whether such errors or omissions result from negligence, accident, or any other cause.

While every effort has been made to avoid any mistake or omission, this publication is being sold on the condition and understanding that neither the author nor the publishers or printers would be liable in any manner to any person by reason of any mistake or omission in this publication or for any action taken or omitted to be taken or advice rendered or accepted on the basis of this work. For any defect in printing or binding the publishers will be liable only to replace the defective copy by another copy of this work then available.

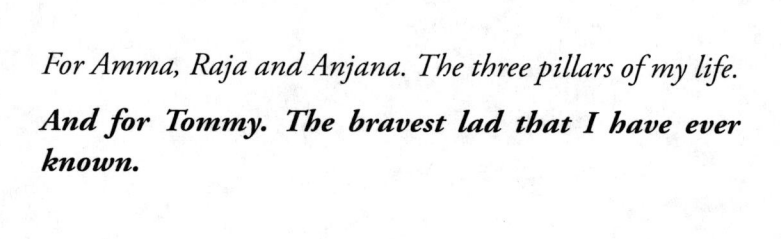

For Amma, Raja and Anjana. The three pillars of my life.

And for Tommy. The bravest lad that I have ever known.

CONTENTS

Author's Note	*7*
Foreword	*11*
1. Coming Back Home	15
2. The Golden Lock	28
3. A Pocket Full Of…	40
4. The Agony of Eviction	50
5. The Teacher	58
6. A Home to Remember	64
7. Parle G	71
8. The Musician and His Muse	76
9. The Teen Bride	87
10. The First-Born	96
11. The Messenger	105
12. Memory Lanes	114
13. Ten Paisa	116
14. Luck, Destiny or Fate?	121
15. One Life, Two Loves	129

Contents

16. The Final Letter	141
17. The First Cut	149
18. The Uninvited Guests	174
19. 13 Days	181
20. Meanderings in the Meadow	197
Acknowledgements	*199*
About the Author	*203*

AUTHOR'S NOTE

As I sat in a quiet café in one of the *ghats* of Benares, typing the two last stories of this book, a friend asked me, "How does it feel to write a book?"

At that point, ideas, words and emotions flooded my mind and I needed them to be poured into the stories. I had no answer for him.

A gratifying meal and three hours of typing followed and I put in the final full stop of my book.

I looked at the time. It was 7:50 p.m. November 8, 2022, a day after Kashi's famed Dev Diwali. I began to write an email to my editor to send across the book.

I paused as realisation hit me. I had finished my first book. I was overwhelmed. Time stood still. I experienced a myriad of beautiful emotions, but what stood out the most was: Gratitude.

Gratitude for life as it has been. For all that I had, all I have and all that I lost. At this moment. For opportunities won and lost.

Every tiny decision, every turn in one's step creates a trajectory that finally determines the life that one lives.

Author's note

This book is significantly different from the one I intended. The initial stories remain the same. A test reader read the first version and told me, "I read all the other stories with a hangover of the initial ones and I could not forget the characters. What happened to them? I want to know more about them."

Those lines led me to rewrite the book focusing on Kala and her family alone.

These stories are a work of fiction, as are the characters. But is not most fiction inspired by real life?

Many of us may know people like Kala, Adhira, Mukundan, Shiva, Raghu and others. Some of my readers may have experienced or heard similar tales at home. I hope they relish these dollops of bittersweet nostalgia, as they walk through these pages and live life momentarily through the characters I created.

Writing a book is truly like taking a precious piece of your soul and smearing it on paper with love. The only difference is, you are still whole, and rather the entire process enriches your core beyond anything you could fathom.

This book is the realisation of a dream I had as a nine-year-old, who spent her free time contemplating whether to become a surgeon who writes or a writer who operates.

Author's note

I wish to whole-heartedly thank every single person who holds this book in their hand or on their kindle. Dear readers, journey the world through the pages of my book and I hope it will be memorable.

– Anuradha

FOREWORD

"We are, as a species, addicted to story. Even when the body goes to sleep, the mind stays up all night, telling itself stories."

– Jonathan Gottschall

Story-telling is a practice exercised by many, though mastered only by a handful. From the musician weaving symphonies out of thin air to the actor portraying the essence of a character through a myriad of expressions; the child caught red-handed with his fist in the candy jar and the medical resident reporting a case in the morning rounds, we are all composers of a wealth of stories. And any writer, whether it is a school-going student penning an essay at the eleventh hour or a prolific journalist with writer's block would attest to the fact that it does not always come easy.

One does not always need to be a gifted scribe, however, to be able to distinguish between good writing and masterful storytelling – a matter of well-chosen words strung together in elegant sentences, versus breathing life into a scene so much so that one becomes a part of the composition. And from the very first tale, it is clear the rare kind of skilful storytelling that Anuradha espouses.

Foreword

The essence of a well-woven tale, in my belief, lies in the strength of its characters – and in this regard, she has left no stone unturned in engendering a variety of wide-ranging personalities. The intense undercurrent of feminism running through the book is underscored by powerful female characters – the penniless young mother, forced to sacrifice the occasional luxury to ensure that her little ones' bellies are full; the young bride who is transported to her childhood through a packet of Parle G biscuits; by touching upon taboo themes such as domestic abuse, sexual assault and even cold murder, it brings into sharp relief the harsh realities forced upon women over generations in a patriarchal society.

Tales of compassion, fortitude and grit interspersed with powerful verses on parental affection and her musings on the sad state of injustice perpetuated against lesser creatures, encompass a rich collection to be devoured over an idle weekend or leafed through one at a time to end a weary day. It can be asserted that Anuradha truly weaves magic with her words and spins stories that stay with the reader long after the last page is turned.

Prof Dr Rohit Shetty

Clinician & Translational scientist

Narayana Nethralaya, Bengaluru

"I suppose in the end, the whole of life becomes an act of letting go, but what always hurts the most is not taking a moment to say goodbye."

— Yann Martel, *Life of Pi*

COMING BACK HOME

The aircraft door opened and as I stood at the exit door, I was welcomed by a gentle humid breeze laced with the exhilarating scent of damp earth and greenery, and a whiff of the sea. I was home.

I felt joy, disappointment, sadness and fear all at once. It was three years since I visited. The last time was when my mother was on her deathbed.

As the white Ambassador car made its way from the airport, I experienced a myriad of emotions, in quick succession: Joy, grief, fear, anxiety, eagerness; but most of all, nostalgia. A lifetime of memories. Some that brought a smile to my face, some tears in my eyes. En route, the familiar greenery warmed my aching heart. I could not rest my mind for a second. I felt numb with the whirlpool of thoughts and emotions running through my mind.

Very soon we were passing through a familiar area.

I could picture the area 45 years ago, walking the same road which was one-third the present size, holding hands with my then-best friend Rameshwari, on our way to school. How I used to love to walk back with her, to her home during lunch break and eat the simple yet tasty lunch cooked by her mother, following which I would grab a piece of sweet cinnamon bark to chew on the way back home.

I wonder where and how Rameshwari was now. I cannot thank her enough, for these are amongst my favourite memories.

College...temple roads...old houses, shops...that bus stop...the flower lady...the palace road...

We passed another familiar area. An area I knew better than the back of my hand. It was on the narrow lane that turned to the right from the main street. This was the first house my family owned, after having lived in dozens of rental places. It was the fourth house on the left and had a large verandah, the *tulsi* plant at the threshold of the house, where *Amma* would draw a *kolam* (pattern of design drawn with rice powder in courtyards in Southern parts of India) every morning on the damp ground, the open area just outside the main door where *Appa* would place his large cane rocking chair and talk to visitors. Large rooms, high ceilings, a spacious courtyard and a well. I was a child when we were evicted from that house. I vividly remember returning home from school to find all the items flung out one by one by strange men and Amma who was expecting what would have been our youngest sibling at that time, crying in the street, surrounded by my older siblings, all looking helpless. That remains the most painful memory of

Coming Back Home

my life, until Amma's death. I never did enter that lane again, after the eviction. The last I heard some years ago from one of my older siblings was that they had broken down the house and a high rise was in the plans at that site.

At Amma's death rites, all her children were present. It was after many years that all of us were under the same roof. And it may easily have been the last time, considering how each of us was scattered across the country and the world, busy with family and work. Each one of us had memories to share, and misunderstandings to clear. When we recollected the first home we owned, there was not one person in the room that did not shed tears.

The car moved along the way, getting closer and closer to the destination, whizzing past shops, buildings, homes, bus stops, tiny hotels, large restaurants, paan shops, and newspaper stands – old and new.

Then came the fields near our home. I recollected my school days, competing with the neighbourhood girls when it came to collecting flowers for Onam, our harvest festival. There was a competition to collect the maximum number of flowers and the rarest ones. After spending hours together plucking flowers at dawn, we would return home with a large basket of flowers in a riot of colours, and a variety of sizes. The tiny yellow-orange ones were the hardest to pluck. One had to be extremely gentle and large quantities were needed.

It was backbreaking work. No wonder, it was left to the youngest in the house! Then we would help our mothers create an ornate pattern with the flowers in the courtyard of the house in front of the main door, as a welcome to our ancient king Bali, who is believed to come and visit our homes on this day. I am certain, half the flowering plant species we would collect as children may have long disappeared with modernization and the destruction of open lands and vegetation.

A childhood undiluted by modern technology, and machinery is a blessing. The children these days playing on their i-pads and mobiles will never realise what they have lost.

We reached the bus stop close to home, where I spent many hours waiting for buses to take me to college. There were two girls dressed in salwar suits, an old woman in a white sari holding a black umbrella, and a young man on a bicycle close by. The young man was not waiting for a bus, but eyeing the prettier one among the two girls, quite to her embarrassment.

Hmmm...times have not changed.

It is hilarious when I come across some of the men who in their youth had waited for me at the bus stop. These men are now married and responsible husbands and fathers, yet embarrassed, they grin awkwardly when they see me.

There, a few minutes before the railway tracks, on the right we passed the hospital where my daughter was born. I spent the next few months at home. The best three months of my life. My daughter was the only grandchild among the many grandchildren, to have been raised at Amma's home.

Someone once told me at a certain age in life, all you have are memories. I guess I am nearing that age.

I was getting closer to home and getting more restless by the minute.

I passed Kuttan, the shopkeeper from whom Amma would buy sweets and bananas every other day and an occasional toy or dress from his limited options for a visiting grandchild.

The car took the final turn off the main road to enter the lane to my home.

The long winding narrow lanes, with twists and turns, adorned on both sides with lovely bamboo fences with wild creepers growing on them ever so gracefully. The tiny mimosa plants on either side bending shyly at the slightest touch, the tiny flowers of myriad colours that were invariably ignored until Onam, when all girls would run out early in the morning to collect every flower, they could lay eyes on. Nothing had changed. Yet something had!

As I saw the iron-rusted gate of the home I grew up in, my heart skipped a beat. Gone was the bamboo fence, and lost was the *henna* creeper that had enriched my hands with lovely patterns for so many joyful years. Instead, a stark grey concrete wall fanned the iron gate.

I could not bring myself to come back to my mother's place these few years. It felt as though the spirit had left, only the body remained. It was not home without Amma.

Finally, at the insistence of my daughter, I forced myself to return, for a short visit. I too felt I needed to reconnect with the place I was born and brought up in. No matter where one lives, the attachment to the land where one is born stays forever.

I stepped out and walked to the gate, opened it and crossed the threshold.

There was the old gap in the wall that opened to the neighbour's courtyard. Chitra, my firstborn, discovered that gap when she was a wild one-year-old, running all over the place, having just learned to walk and run. I can still hear her squeals of laughter at her find. Every time she was missing from the courtyard, I would have to go to our neighbour's home to get her back. No one older than five could pass through that gap. Despite all the years, the opening which kept growing larger and larger remained. This was an obvious insight into the great relationship we had with our neighbours. Such wonderful kind people. Their children and our kids still keep moving to and fro through the opening, equally welcome at both homes.

Coming Back Home

Typically, I would expect to see a clean courtyard, with a freshly painted *kolam* that still showed signs of imperfection in the form of a few lines that never were straight despite years of practice.

Today, there were leaves strewn all over. No trace of a kolam. No one had drawn a kolam for a while, as a kolam always leaves a mark even if it's a few days old.

I took a deep breath and swallowed my emotions and firmly told myself to be strong.

This was the second home we owned and I was in college when we bought this land. I watched the house being built, brick by brick. All the fights I had with Appa on the architectural plan were so worthy. We lived in a makeshift hutment in the back while the construction was going on. And oh my, what a beautiful house it grew to be! Pristine white walls, brick red smooth floor, red-tiled roof, high ceiling. How happy we were and how proud! Each plant and tree in the courtyard had a story, like every brick in the house.

I walked ahead and as I neared my front door, I glanced at the two neem trees beyond, in the backyard. I wanted to see a freshly washed nine-yards silk sari wrapping the two trees and tied with a single knot, left out to dry. A sight I was accustomed to seeing all my life. A sight that gave me a sense of security – of knowing I was home, of knowing that mother is at home.

But, the two trees were bare and lifeless without my mother's sari. The leaves were brown and were falling. It appeared that even their spirits had departed along with Amma.

Amma was not here anymore. The feeling hit me hard and I did not attempt to hold back my tears.

Through the hazy view from my teary eyes, I reached for the front door, which was always unlocked except at night.

I saw my elder brother sitting on a chair. He looked up, our eyes met and not a word was spoken for a long time. My tears were answered by his.

I went to the room that was my mother's. It was still Amma's room. It was kept intact. Except for the fact, that the cupboard lay empty save for two of her sarees, a blouse and a bedsheet. Gone was the tiny carved wooden box where she kept her prescriptions and the only gold chain she owned. The bed had not been slept in for three years.

There was the iron nail on the wall where my daughter's first-ever bangle hung. Now the bangle was missing and the nail lay bare.

Each year when we visited, Amma would put it on my daughter's hand to see how far it fit. When she was two months old, the bangle reached up to her shoulder. As she grew, it reached her elbow, her wrist, then four fingers and on the last visit it fit a knuckle and a half.

Coming Back Home

Every time Amma would chuckle and say, "Now it will not fit you, Chitra!"

In that same room, there was a shelf that belonged to my brother, the only sibling among nine who lived with Amma until her very end. My brother was possessive of his belongings. When I was in college, I would steal his film magazines to read them in secret. I am not sure whether he ever found out, as when I would place them back, I would ensure it was placed just as perfectly, not one magazine out of line. Everything on that shelf was arranged at right angles to each other. While my cupboard would be a mess, in contrast, much to Amma's displeasure. My younger daughter Lakshmi did inherit Amma's melodious singing voice. I often ask her to sing for me. Raising children is a hard task. Wonder how Amma did not go crazy raising nine kids, each one a world apart from the previous. Or maybe she did.

I walked to the kitchen to find that the spacious kitchen lay bare. The walls were coated in soot near the cooking area, a mark left behind by a minor mishap that occurred a few years ago. This is where Amma spent a major portion of her life. The kitchen seemed ignored. That is when I realized that my brother looked thinner than he had ever been in his life.

In the right corner of the floor, below the wooden shelves lay the stone mortar and pestle. The mortar and pestle were used for making curry powder, and chutneys daily and occasionally for grinding freshly plucked henna leaves for applying *mehendi* on our hands.

Those occasions when Amma would apply mehendi on my hands were always very special. I always felt like a princess and the luckiest person on earth. Amma was truly special. I knew this right from the start.

She was a gifted cook. Anything she touched would be befitting of kings and emperors. She did learn the art of cooking well, as in her childhood she was accustomed to eating food from the royal palace. The neighbourhood was always in praise of her curries. She was an expert in various Ayurvedic concoctions, which she would painstakingly prepare to perfect proportions whenever she would hear of any suffering in the area. Women would always walk into our home to meet Amma for advice on various issues, ranging from cooking to managing their families. We, her children at times would joke, that it was only us that did not go to her for advice ever.

The large hibiscus plant stood in the middle of our backyard. It would always be laden with more flowers than it could carry. Now it appeared to have stopped flowering.

The backyard was a wilderness.

The backyard fire which would be smouldering lay cold and damp.

Coming Back Home

The house was empty. It was not home anymore. Just a memory. Memories that would last a lifetime. That made life worthwhile.

My brother and I spoke for hours on length. We took all the old photographs from the attic and cupboard and went through them. Amma looked so beautiful. Even at the ripe old age of 92, she looked as my father had described her when they were newlywed, "Your Mother looked as beautiful as a lit lamp in a dark room."

I went for a walk afterwards. I walked along familiar pathways and met friendly neighbours who had such wonderful memories of Amma, many that I heard for the first time. Few young mothers looked as lost as me. I realized how much Amma meant to the entire neighbourhood. I reached Sharada Amma's home. She was Amma's close friend. I entered to find her lying on a bamboo mat on the floor, weak from old age more than disease. I called out to her and sat on the floor. It took her a while to get adjusted to the dim light in the room and recognise me. "Mithila, is that you?" I nodded as she spoke falteringly.

"Kala has left us. I have no one to speak to now. My time too is nearing. Nice of you to visit."

With each word, her strength seemed to be failing. As I bid a sad farewell, I met her son on stepping out. He mentioned how her health had suddenly taken a turn for the worse after Amma's death.

I continued walking. I reached the rail track where I had caught Raghu, the youngest amongst us sitting on a rock, having bunked school. Long, long ago. What a whacking he had received that day. Amma was merciless. Raghu too, like me, had stopped visiting home since Amma passed away. The younger children were closer to Amma, and her passing away affected us more deeply it seems.

Beyond the rail track, was the bridge where we would go often. I would take my daughters here each time we visited. The sunset over the still backwaters, adorned with palm trees and coconut trees with an occasional boat, was a sight to behold from the bridge. Never failing to mesmerize even if you would see it every single day. I miss home and Kerala.

I moved farther along and reached the Devi temple, which Amma would frequently visit. She would pray for her nine children and 15 grandchildren on their birthdays, which she never forgot. It was believed in the neighbourhood that all her prayers are always answered, being a pious Brahmin lady. We were witnesses to that. Not one prayer of hers would go unanswered. Such was her faith. I looked at the golden sand on the temple grounds, and wondered to myself, how many times Amma had walked on these sand grains. I felt tears streaming down my face. The cool evening breeze in vain tried to dry them. I did not enter the temple and retraced my steps back home.

Coming Back Home

After a quiet dinner with my brother, I bid him farewell. And asked him to visit me whenever he wished to. I knew he would not leave home easily, even for a few days. Nevertheless.

As I was leaving, I turned back to see if I could see a slim graceful beautiful woman draped in a silk nine-yards sari, with her long white flowing hair tied loosely in a bun, with a single gold bangle in her right hand standing against the door waving goodbye.

There was no one.

I sat in the car, and as the car sped away, I kept looking behind for the same woman to walk out on the lane and wave goodbye and stand there till the car was out of sight.

Only this time there was no one.

THE GOLDEN LOCK

"Please Amma, please. It's only two rupees. I will never ask you for money again. Please Amma...", cried little Raghu, stomping his tiny legs that were covered in sand and bruises that were in various stages of healing as always. Clad in his school uniform – Prussian blue shorts, frayed at the edges and a white shirt that was brown with mud stains and beginning to show signs of wear and tear, he followed his dear mother from room to room. His wide teary eyes and the tear tracks on his dirty face that ran down the side of his nose, to the corners of his mouth, ending at the protruding prominent chin, did not seem to soften his mother's stand. His mother could buy a week's ration to feed her large family with that money.

Little Raghu was the youngest of nine siblings. Life was bittersweet. Being the youngest he was the most pampered, yet had to face the heat from every member in the house at the slightest mischief. And when it came to mischief, his imagination never disappointed him. A bright student, yet he would be seen standing outside class, with his hands holding his ears almost every day. Incessant complaints from his teachers would infuriate his elder sister who was in the same school – a calm and docile young girl – who was forever trying

The Golden Lock

to withhold the reputation and respect of the family name. She lost count of the number of times she had found Raghu wandering along the rail tracks or playing and rolling thin rubber tyres down the road, instead of going to school. Disobedient, easily distracted, and very naughty, yet she could not name one person on Earth she loved more than Raghu.

Every year the school took students for a picnic. The students, who could afford the minimal rate charged went, while the rest of the students eagerly waited at their homes, looking forever out of their windows for the school friend who would walk along the path outside their homes. Raghu thus had already spent last year looking out of the window on the day of the class picnic. After a long wait, late in the evening when an exhausted Gopal dragged his muddy self home, Raghu ran out and excitedly asked the reluctant Gopal to spill every tiny detail about the trip. Gopal described the bus ride to the beautiful temple that they visited in a quaint village in rural Kerala and how they pitched in the mango grove, climbed trees, threw stones, and shook the trees to bring down the sweet, luscious, juicy, orange-red mangoes, played and ran till their tiny feet could take no more. Raghu's eyes grew wider with each description and he keenly wished he could have been there with his best friends. How he would have played with Gopal, Sethu and Vineet!

This year, it was during the Mathematics class taught by Susamma, that the class teacher, Leela, announced the picnic. Until then Raghu was busy playing around with his slate and chalk, breaking the chalk into tiny bits and throwing it at Revathi, much to her annoyance. The word picnic brought Raghu back into the present and the memories of the past year came back to him. He was not going to be the one to miss out on all the fun this year. This time the picnic was planned to a waterfall that was famous for its massive size and height. It was a favoured picnic spot for many. The water thundered down many feet and turned calm and then flowed in a gentle stream. It was here that families set up their picnic baskets and children and adults alike took pleasure in the pristine fresh and clear stream that nature had gifted. The entire region, like most of Kerala, was blessed with abundant greenery and flora. The cost of the trip was two rupees per student, which would include lunch and two biscuits at breakfast and on the journey back.

Thus, a highly determined Raghu who was all of seven years, walked barefooted the entire five km from his school to his house, in double quick time, as fast as his legs could carry him. He did not greet the shopkeeper, who sold his favourite orange candy, nor did he wave to Amu *akka* at the flower shop, he even ran past Gopal before Gopal could call out to him.

Raghu continued running behind his beloved Amma, crying out for two rupees, for a long time. Kala ran the family on a tight budget. Her husband being away working in Bombay, the responsibility of running

The Golden Lock

the family on her husband's meagre salary, lay entirely on her shoulders. The memory of her eviction when she was pregnant was still fresh in her mind. She would never forgive her husband for losing the only home they ever owned. She also lost their last child as she had gone into premature labour right after that incident.

The present house was too small for the army of children and her. Yet she was happy with the fact that her fourth son, a keen farmer could grow most of the vegetables needed for daily cooking. Blessed is the soil in Kerala, where any seed randomly strewn out the window, would emerge into a beautiful tree in no time at all.

Kala never regretted the fact that she seldom brought her children new clothes. None of them had shoes and they never asked for any either. They walked for miles each day without a thought of any alternative. She was a proud woman nevertheless. No one went hungry in her home. Never.

But the house rent bore heavily on her and the rations like rice, oil, and milk could not be grown in their backyard. She saved every little penny. She made certain she would never have to be thrown out due to non-payment of rent. She dreamed of owning a home again. Only that would dim, if not erase the pain of losing the beautiful one they had owned.

Her youngest born's intense desire to go on a school picnic did not make her relent as she could not afford the price. Picnics were luxuries that only the children of the rich could afford, said Kala. Her firm stance and short temper did not dissuade Raghu from stepping back and he pursued her despite the number of times she whacked him out of exasperation. She eventually gave up and, in a bid, to get him out of the house told him, "You need money. Go and pray to Lord Krishna. He will send you on the picnic if you deserve to go!" Kala was a God-fearing woman who derived her strength through her unbreakable faith and fervent prayers.

Raghu's eyes, which had become puffy and swollen with the crying, suddenly widened and he looked at his Amma and asked, "Krishna will help me Amma?" Kala, already tired with several problems running through her restless mind, absent-mindedly replied, "Yes, yes. Pray with all your heart and complete seven *pradakshinas* (circumambulations) around the temple".

Raghu knew the temple his mother favoured the most. Without much ado, he walked bare-footed the seven km to the temple.

Even though he was only seven, in these few years, Raghu had unknowingly learnt lessons that would take a lifetime to learn. He learnt not to take anything for granted. Whatever he had today, he could lose tomorrow. So, he was happy with any toy that he received and would play with it the entire day, before his brothers came and snatched it away. He learnt to

The Golden Lock

sneak into the kitchen at odd hours, when his mother was asleep and stealthily pick out the precious grated coconut or jaggery, fill in his pockets and just as silently get out of the house to a safe corner in the wilderness of the courtyard to enjoy his treat, albeit with a tinge of fear, that his mother would soon realize and give him a well-deserved, resounding spanking and a tinge of guilt, that the curry the next day for the entire family would be deficient in richness due to the lesser amount of coconut.

Being the youngest, one could say Raghu was the most loved yet the most bullied too. And he did bear the brunt of having lived through some of the toughest days the family faced, monetarily.

After a long trek, he arrived at the temple. The sun had begun its descent. He was dwarfed in front of the majestic carved wooden doorway with golden handles that was opened each morning before the first rays of the sun hit the earth on this side of the world. Not even the most beautiful, poetic words could describe the grace of the temple and its premises.

As one neared the temple one could see the 22 feet tall lamp. Beyond that was the inner doorway and the tall powerful pillars arranged symmetrically, adorning the opening to the inner sanctum of the temple. The perfect congruency showed the mastery of the architect (whose picture can be seen just by entering the outer gate of the temple) and the artisans. The large temple with its rectangular format had lamps on all walls, which when lit during festivals in the evening would be a sight to behold, one that would warm the heart and fill the mind with peace in the most tumultuous of times. In the innermost part of the temple, the scent of burning oil lamps and camphor and sandalwood paste welcomed the devotees. The evening *aarti* (prayer ritual) was a sight to behold, to witness the idols of various Gods decked in their finest and grandest.

But Raghu was quite oblivious to the beauty of the temple at that tender age and his favourite area of the temple was the courtyard. Sandalwood-coloured sand filled the massive courtyard grounds. A stone pathway in the centre was placed in a circular format. As Raghu took his first step onto the sand with his right foot, as always instructed by his Amma, he felt the tiny stones in the otherwise fine sand prick underneath his feet. A few more steps and his feet got accustomed to the prickly stones beneath. He folded his hands the moment he stepped into the inner sanctum and prayed fervently to the Gods to grant him the opportunity to go to the picnic. He paid a visit to every God in the temple premises and then began the pradakshinas around the temple. Seven times, as his Amma instructed. He repeatedly chanted the same *mantra*, not losing focus for a single second, "Oh Lord, please let me go for the school picnic...Please, dear Krishna!"

The sun had set by the time he was halfway through his third pradakshina. The priests were busy lighting lamps around the temple. The already beautiful structure looked magical with the addition of Lord Agni (Lord of Fire), adorning it with various lamps. On completion of the stipulated seven pradakshinas, Raghu made his way home, feeling a bit hopeful. After all, how unkind could the Gods be to an innocent boy with a simple wish?

Kala had finished preparing dinner: parboiled rice, *sambar, rasam, kootu,* beans curry, *poppadums* and salted buttermilk. She called the children to dinner. One call from her, and everyone sat down for dinner. As she began serving, she noticed Raghu was missing. The friendly village was a place where children seldom stayed home and roamed around freely playing in the pathways and neighbourhood courtyards all day. She was worried as this was too late an hour for him not to return. Plus, the tantrum he threw for the picnic money got her very worried. She served food to the other children, ages ranging from 11 to 25 years and then went out, opened the gate and stood on the narrow road bordered with henna creepers and bamboo fences on either side and kept looking anxiously into the distance for the sight of a little boy coming home. Time passed, and a car tried to squeeze its way through the narrow lane. The car appeared mammoth-like as it made its way, its tyres squishing the shrubbery on either side of the lane. As it came nearer, Kala recognised it as her elder brother's. She was pleasantly surprised since not only was the hour late, but her brother seldom visited her. It was she who would frequent his spacious bungalow for milk or an occasional loan. Kala was a dignified woman who never liked unnecessary favours. Mostly she would be called upon to cook at festivals for guests. The siblings had an unusual relationship. The rich-poor divide had taken precedence over warm sibling camaraderie. She knew he found it beneath his status to come to her humble abode and she had long since stopped inviting him over. Nevertheless, she was at her politest best when the car door opened and a well-built man a few inches over five feet, on the heavier side emerged, wearing a silk *dhoti* and a pristine white shirt buttoned to the collar, a gold chain just peeking out, at the nape, and blue *chappals* and a polished wooden walking stick – more of a style statement than a sign of any disability. He casually walked towards Kala. Neither smiled or exchanged greetings. She asked him to come inside. He noticed the children and seeing the youngest one with the largest eyes, was missing asked, "Kalavati, where is the little devil?" Kala decided to hide her anxiety and said, "He has gone to the neighbour's home and will be back any minute." She did not want her brother to think of her as an inefficient or careless mother. Hearing her actual name warmed her heart though. Only her mother used to call her Kalavati. She was Kala to the rest.

He sat in the sole chair in their living room while the children finished dinner.

"Will you have dinner?"

"No."

"Shall I make coffee?"

"No."

He sat in silence while Kala stood against the wall to his left. Nobody spoke for quite a while. Finally, he lamented, "I was passing by and thought I should visit you."

Silence.

"Shalini said it's been a while since you came home. I wanted to make sure everything is all right."

Kala was surprised. After all these years, hearing the confession of an endearing emotion like a worry for a sibling, was unheard of and unexpected from her brother. Shalini, her sister-in-law would miss her only when it came to the laborious task of cooking for 60 people during *bhajans* organised at their home. During these events, not once did they invite her children. Her children and his children never played together. Her nieces and nephews would never acknowledge her children as cousins. But Kala never took it to heart. Circumstances change in life. It was God's will. His rule.

"We eat. Three meals. Each day."

Silence.

The only sounds now heard were that of the crickets hiding in the grass in the backyard. The night air was cool without any breeze. The leaves were still.

Moonlight shone through the leaves leaving patterns on the ground, like a beautiful black and grey abstract carpet.

Kala was now extremely worried about her darling, her youngest and wondered if she should have dealt with him more kindly.

"All right then. I have to take leave. It's late."

He stood up and walked to the door. Kala followed him, all the while bewildered by his visit and worried sick about Raghu. The car door was opened by the driver. Kala kept stealing glances to the end of the road, praying she would see her little boy. To her relief, she saw him. Raghu was walking slowly towards her. He seemed tired and she noticed blisters on his feet. As her brother was just about to get into the white Ambassador car, he caught a glimpse of the tiny figure walking towards them. He closed the car door gently and waited for the young boy.

"You little devil! How long do you play?"

He reached into his shirt pocket, grabbed something and placed it in Raghu's palm, did not say another word and got into his car.

As the car sped off, Kala caught hold of Raghu, in a moment of relief, held him close.

"Where have you been silly boy? You had me so worried! Next time you get home this late, I will whack you."

The Golden Lock

Raghu held her hand and rested his head against her. He was very tired.

"Wash your hands and feet. Eat dinner before you go to bed."

Absent-mindedly Raghu went to wash his hands at the outdoor basin. As he was about to wash his hand, he opened his palm, which was still holding what his uncle gave him. It was a brand new two-rupee note.

Raghu gasped. Ran back to his Amma, and hugged her tight.

"Raghu, you still have not washed your hands! What did I just tell you to do?"

"Amma, look what *mama* (maternal uncle) gave me!"

For the first time in many months did Kala see such joy radiate in her boy's eyes. For once she was thankful to her brother. She had never known her brother to be so generous before. The tightness of the embrace from that little being was enough for her to feel happiness, which she had not felt in a long while.

She cleaned up her boy, fed him with her hands and gave him an extra banana, which he was so fond of.

That night Raghu slept peacefully with the money tucked safely under his pillow, dreaming of a majestic wooden doorway with a golden lock and a magnificent idol seated within….

A POCKET FULL OF...

It was a dark night. One could hear the silence crackle through the sinister darkness. The silence was interrupted by the dry leaves crushed under feet and the occasional hoot of an owl. The lone Brahmin held his account book closer to his chest, quickening his pace with every step. He repeatedly tried to push away his wife's warning voice in his head, "Leave the meeting on time. It is dangerous to come alone through the woods after dusk." Not one to pay heed to her words, he hoped he would not regret it this time.

Long was the walk to his house. He wished he had not tarried behind in the merriments after the meeting. But how could he have helped it, if the dancer was so beautiful? After her performance, in which she seduced the entire audience with her facial gestures and hip movements, she was showered with money and praises by the leering men, the corners of their mouths dribbling with red-brown juice of *paan* (Indian betel leaf folded over a mixture of betel nut, spices and lime).

It was past dusk when Girishgiri began to trace his steps home to a more laidback and disciplined life. His wife's incessant nagging would welcome him back to his true senses, away from the din and jubilation at

A Pocket Full of...

the meet. For a man up-to-date with the entrant and skill of any new dancer or entertainer in town, he had witnessed a performance after quite a while, by his standards.

A clerk with a local moneylender, he was skilled at his job. A devout Hindu, he would start his day with prayers and a visit to the Vishnu temple near their home. Then he would be at work submerged in papers and bills till dusk. A serious man, the only time he was seen letting his hair down was during the dance recitals of the latest entertainer in town. That was his only vice.

Girishgiri began chanting Vishnusahasranam to ward off any evil as the darkness crept around him. As he moved deeper into the woods, his voice was the only sound breaking into the stillness. An occasional breeze would cause a twig to crackle, sending shivers down his spine and a tremor in his speech. After a while, he sensed something amiss. He slowed down and lowered his chanting. He could hear footsteps behind him. He went silent and started to walk again. The footsteps began as soon as he resumed walking. These steps were soft and gentle, unlike his harsh ones that caused the dried leaves to crumble beneath his heavy tread.

After a few minutes of stopping, listening and walking again, which was mimicked by the other creature; he was terrified and turned around and screamed, "Who's there?"

A profound silence followed. He started to walk, only to hear the footsteps again. Now it seemed to get closer to him. On reaching a clearing where the moonlight shone brightly, he picked up a large fallen branch, off the muddy ground and gathered every ounce of courage in his being asked, "Whoever it is, I am not scared of you. Come forward and show yourself!"

The footsteps came closer and closer. Now Girishgiri could hear the clinking sound of anklets, along with the rustling leaves and breeze. Very soon out of the dark woods emerged a creature in white. As it got closer, to his relief and delight, it was a woman. In the moonlight, he admired her ravishing beauty. The wide forehead, kohl-lined, dark, doe-shaped eyes, the aquiline nose, the perfectly shaped luscious quivering lips displaying a deep shade of pink and the protruding chin. Her long slender neck and fair skin were complemented by long shapely fingers. The white sari with golden embroidery draped to perfection clung to her shapely hips. Never being one to resist beauty, Girishgiri forgot the fear that had engulfed him a few moments ago. A visibly excited Girishgiri asked the young woman, "My dear lady, what are you doing in the deep woods all alone at this ungodly hour?"

The woman, fidgeting with the sari *pallu* (the end of a sari that flows over from the shoulder), spoke reticently at first and shyly, "Dear Sir, I was returning home, but then I got lost and after walking for a long while I am glad to have come across another human."

A Pocket Full of…

"The woods are not safe, my lady. Not for one as young and beautiful as you. Don't you worry, I shall safely escort you home," said the gallant Girishgiri.

"Thank you, Sir. I shall forever be in debt to you for this kindness."

Soon, both of them started to walk on the same path. Girishgiri was far from his previous nervousness and asked the woman extensively about her whereabouts. She belonged to an aristocratic family from the neighbouring town and was on her way to visit her relatives in this town.

He asked her if she was a dancer to which she replied affirmatively. On questions of marriage, he learnt that she was not engaged yet.

As they walked along, the woman who was lagging a few steps behind him for the past hour, now walked alongside him. As they walked, the night became sinister, and Girishgiri felt her hand brush against his a few times. He assumed it must be by accident, not that he was complaining. As they reached a clearing and came to the crossroads, the woman told him that there was a house close by and that they could go there and wait till sunrise. Reading deeper into her invitation, Girishgiri eagerly nodded and followed her.

He followed her for what seemed a long time. Girishgiri was too mesmerised by her beauty and grace and the soft clinking of her anklets to notice where they were going. She turned around abruptly and offered him a *paan*. He accepted it and put the betel leaf quid into the corner of his mouth. As he was chewing on the juicy pan, it dawned upon him that this woman was not carrying any box or package in her hand. He wondered from where she had produced this *paan* or where she stored it. But he didn't dwell too long on that. After all, how many times in his life did he have the privilege of the company of such a dainty maiden?

She seemed to walk fast now. He had to run to keep pace. He was perplexed, she walked slowly but the distances she covered were more than the length of her steps and speed. He looked down at her feet, hoping to distract himself by catching a glimpse of her delicate ankles. Her sari was too long and did not show her feet. Then a cool night breeze came by and the sari lifted a bit. Girishgiri was surprised to note that she seemed to walk a few inches above the ground. Was he imagining things? Or was it the intoxicating juice of the betel nut playing tricks on his mind?

He convinced himself he was out of his mind and decided to walk on ignoring his imagination. They walked a long way, with her gracefully covering great distances, and he running after her, catching his breath and still unable to keep up.

They reached a palm grove in the middle of the deep woods. The woman in white turned around slowly. Girishgiri had to suddenly stop in his tracks to avoid banging into her. She put forth her white arm, her long slender fingers open towards the sky, and coyly asked, "Dear Sir, could you spare me a betel leaf?"

Girishgiri caught off guard, nodded vigorously and fumbled with his iron box where he carefully stored select betel leaves, nuts and lime. He took out a betel leaf and awkwardly balanced it in one hand, clumsily applied the lime on the leaf, placed a few nuts on it, folded it carefully and offered it to her. She placed the leaf in her mouth, against her right cheek. Girishgiri noticed that her skin was whiter than he first thought, unusually pale in the moonlight in the palm grove. As she swallowed the juice from the leaf, she smiled at him. For reasons unknown, he had an eerie feeling. A smile such as this would have been deemed very inviting in any other situation. It must have been the dead silence and the woods, he thought. In the stillness, another gust of wind blew, and Girishgiri happened to glance down, to avoid the dust carried by the wind.

He was profoundly perplexed when he noticed her feet were oddly placed with toes pointing back and the heels in front. And she was standing a few inches above the ground. Girishgiri broke out into a sweat and all of a sudden was aware that he had ventured into the deepest part of the woods, in the area of the palm grove that long was dreaded and infamous because of legends of supernatural creatures living on the palm trees. The trees were more closely placed, the paths non-existent.

No human seemed to have traversed these areas in years.

He stopped in his tracks and stammered, "Who... who are you? Wha...what do you want?"

The woman in white began to glide in circles around him, rising higher as she did so. Her mesmerising features now did not seem as beautiful. The eyes were turning redder by the minute, the nose longer and sharper, and the protruding chin shooting forward at a very sharp angle. Her skin was as white as that of a ghost, her lips blood red. The woman smiled revealing her sharp canines which grew longer even as he watched till they almost reached her chin.

Girishgiri screamed, "*Yakshi*! *Yakshi*! God, save me!" he held his *dhoti* and ran.

The next morning a rude knock awakened Sumati and her two children. She got up expecting her indifferent husband, ready to give him a piece of her mind for disappearing for the entire night. "He must have stayed back at that dancer's place. Useless man!" The door opened, but it was not her husband. It was the milkman and he was late.

Sumati waited the entire day for Girishgiri. Close to sunset, she went to the town council to report her husband was missing. A search party went into the woods.

A Pocket Full of...

Early the next morning, Sumati was led into the woods by some townsfolk.

There deep, deep in the woods beneath a palm tree in the palm grove, lay some fingernails and hair, of what appeared to be the remains of a human. There was no trace of flesh or bone. No trace of any clothes. A few feet away lay a betel leaf box half open, with its contents strewn across the grounds.

"All right now. That's enough for the day. Time to sleep."

"Akka, where does one find these yakshis? Do they harm little children?"

"No. They target men. You are never to give them any betel leaf when they ask. If you do, you have accepted their invitation to be their next meal."

"Is there no way to avoid them akka?"

"Raghu, enough of your incessant questions! I told you that this tale is not for children. And now you are scared. You never listen. You are so stubborn!"

"Akka, please tell me... please. I beg you Mithila akka! I will not ask any more questions."

"Yakshis do not exist Raghu! They are a part of folklore to tell men not to wander after dark in dangerous lonely places. Yet I will tell you. It is said that the yakshis are terrified of the metal iron.

So, men travelling through woods late at night carry an iron piece in their pocket. The very touch of iron can destroy a yakshi, it is believed. Good night now. Sleep. Wake up early to do your Maths homework."

Five-year-old Raghu curled up against his mother and held her tight looking into the dark room to see if anything was amiss or if any creature would creep up at night.

In the morning, everyone went to school and their usual routine. Evening time on returning, their mother welcomed them with warm glasses of milk and bananas.

It was playtime in the evening. All the kids from the neighbourhood gathered in the largest courtyard in the area. Raghu arrived later than usual at the scene. While playing that day, Raghu seemed very clumsy, unlike his usual self. As he rushed past his sisters to catch a ball, they noted he was holding up his shorts each time he was running. And a clinking sound could be heard. His sisters cornered him, "Raghu, what in the world is in your pocket?"

"Nothing!"

They ran behind him. Raghu gave a good chase, holding his shorts up high and the clinking sound grew louder as he ran faster.

Mithila caught up with him, pinned him down and emptied his heavy pockets to find 20 iron nails in them.

That evening the entire household had a good laugh at the little boy's expense. "Ha ha ha... Raghu thinks a yakshi is going to get him. Ha ha…"

"Amma, if iron items are missing in the house, you know whose pockets to check!"

His elder brother Rama, brought a white towel from the cupboard, draped it on his head, made a wicked face with his teeth protruding and ran behind Raghu, screaming in a high-pitched voice, "I am going to eat you...! I am hungry for blood!"

Raghu felt annoyed, and victimised and ran to his mother, the only sanctuary he had at this moment. Amma shouted at them saying that it was one thing to scare a poor little boy with such stories and worse to make fun of him later. The bullying continued until Amma brought the reliable broomstick which drove everybody out!

Raghu didn't sleep well for a week. After which he was back to his routine mischievous ways.

The long-forgotten iron nails lay in the backyard shed.

THE AGONY OF EVICTION

"Enough! Will you stop that, you stupid boy?" Mithila ran as fast as she could to get away from him, yet she was too late. Rama jumped into the pool of muddy water, splashing her already-soaked uniform. Kerala was always the first to welcome the monsoon rains that hit the country.

The parched earth soaked up the water like a sponge. The trees washed off their dirt and grime, looked newly decked and draped in bridal greenery. The petrichor infused with the perfume of the fallen bed of flowers added to the everlasting charm of rains in God's own country.

Heavy rains terrified the adults but delighted the schoolchildren. All the more reason for causing floods, forcing the schools to declare holidays and in so doing no homework!

Today was one such day. Midway through the second period, the teacher received a message telling her to send the children home, as more heavy rain was predicted promising to drench the entire town and flood the streets as per the weather forecast.

The unexpected half-day holiday drew shrieks and shouts of pure joy as the school children scrambled to

The Agony Of Eviction

pack their bags and the happy faces rushed to the gates in the rain. Most of the children walked to school, no matter how far off their homes might be.

Mithila waited for her elder brother Rama at the school gate daily after school was over and they walked back home together. They walked at a faster pace today. Mithila would often forget to carry an umbrella, just as she did today. When it rained heavily, she would take shelter in shops along the streets while Rama played in the rain and jumped into every single pothole on the way.

Mithila was seven years old while Rama was ten.

They walked the routine eight km till they reached the lane dotted by mimosa plants on both sides and fences covered with henna creepers. The fourth house on the left was home. Mithila had lost count of the number of houses they had moved. But this was the first one they owned while the previous ones were all rented. Among all houses she had lived in her short life; this one was her favourite. It would remain so for the rest of her life.

Many decades later when she would bring her daughters to visit the land of her birth and childhood and youth, she would never step into this lane, but simply peer into the crooked entrance to the lane, as she passed by.

The children trudged along, drenched. They pushed past a few people who were peering above the

Stories My Grandma Never Told Me

gates to open it, and the entire spacious bungalow and lusciously green courtyard came into view.

Today the scene was not as quiet as on other days. It took a few moments for the two children to fathom what was happening. There was a sizable crowd around the house fencing and walls, watching the happenings inside. A woman's pleading voice and an infant's shrieks could be heard above the din of low hustling male voices and steel vessels clanging against the earth.

Mithila and Rama recognized the voice to be that of their dear mother. Amma was seven months pregnant with what would have been their youngest sibling and she held two-year-old Raghu in her arms.

Their mother, Kala was considered to be the most graceful and beautiful woman in the neighbourhood and family. She was blessed with features that no painter could do justice to —large doe-shaped eyes, a perfect nose with a soft tip, high cheekbones and an almond-shaped petite face and a slim figure, except for her present swollen belly despite having nine children and expecting her tenth.

Today she looked different. Her long black hair was untied, flowing till it reached below her hips, and her nine-yard silk sari was not draped as meticulously and gracefully as it was usually. The older children recognised the emotions on her gentle face: a sense of fear, anger, betrayal, hate and hopelessness. She was carrying Raghu with one hand while with the other

The Agony Of Eviction

she was trying to hold on to the shirts of the strange men who kept going into the house and throwing out the items and furniture onto the courtyard.

Her pleas were loud and resounded in the crowd that was unusually quiet and indifferent.

The pleas of a heavily pregnant woman with an infant and four school-going children fell on deaf ears. Everyone had simply come to watch the drama and not help.

Adhira came rushing towards Rama and Mithila. Adhira was in her senior year in school. She dragged the two to the back of the house, seated them on the verandah and quickly went into the kitchen and came out with two plates of rice, sambar and vegetable curry. She asked the children to eat and not ask questions and not worry. She rushed back to be with her mother.

Mithila, years later, would remember the taste of every morsel of this last meal they had in this beautiful house.

The children ate with difficulty sensing fear and sadness. Tears flowed from their eyes despite not completely having understood the situation. They knew their mother was in distress and the men were harassing them and throwing them out of their home.

Adhira returned to take away their plates. It was quiet now. The onlookers had left as well. Adhira had four or five bags with her. She seemed to have packed whatever she could. The *puttu* vessel (a metal kettle with a cylindrical contraption used to prepare the Kerala dish called puttu of rice powder and grated coconut) could be seen peeking out of one bag. She asked the children to come with her carrying their school bags.

Years later, what Mithila distinctly remembered of that fateful evening was that they had walked many miles all day long. Her pregnant mother, Adhira, Rama, Raghu and herself. She vividly recollected reaching the houses of three of her uncles, and each one of them refusing to help them and shutting their door on them.

Her brother added some details of that day when she grew up. Kala walked the bunch to the telegram office to send a message to their father and elder siblings in Mumbai regarding the tragedy and asking a few questions too. Why had he mortgaged the house and not mentioned it to Kala? Who would now take care of their well-being and safety? Only questions remained and her irresponsible husband would not bother to answer or be held accountable for them.

What hurt Mithila the most about this tragedy and memory was the sight of her mother's bare feet, having walked miles with that large belly and Raghu in her arms. To this day, she could not bear to talk of that day without breaking down.

Kala ran helter-skelter into many lanes after failing to get help from her brothers. It was nearly dusk. The children were hungry and she had not eaten a morsel

The Agony Of Eviction

nor had a drop of water since breakfast. Her feet began to ache.

Kala did what she always would during times she felt lost. She took the family to the Devi temple she visited every morning. The temple priest saw her state and didn't try to rush her despite closing hours. Kala had the children wait inside the premises with the few bags she managed to save and pack. She walked into the temple and threw her only two gold bangles at the feet of the goddess. Those were the only gifts she had from her mother to remember her by. She prayed and cried.

The chief priest entered the inner sanctum and offered her *prasaadam* (offerings of temple rituals).

She walked around the temple for a long time and returned to her children seemingly composed. She was convinced the goddess would now take charge of her and her family.

They were leaving and were at the gates of the temple when the priest called out to her. He gave her back her bangles and asked her to meet Govindan Nair at Eroor near the ayurvedic dispensary. Kala thanked him. The family walked the distance to Eroor, Tripunithura.

Govindan Nair was surprised when he heard a knock on his door so late in the evening.

In the next 40 minutes, Kala and her children found themselves in a tiny room. This room would be home for the next few years. Nair was a kind man and he did not ask Kala for any advance payment. Nair's wife gave the family rice and curry for the night, along with drinking water. They had to use a common bathroom that was a little away from the room. That night Kala had her first glass of water in 12 hours. She stretched her weary legs. Her back hurt. She cradled her stomach and wondered what sort of hell this child was being born into. Her feet were swollen and Adhira covered her feet with a damp cloth.

The area where we were now was not one that Brahmins preferred to reside in. Kala knew she would hear comments from her brothers and the community regarding how a Brahmin woman could stay in a locality where people from other castes lived. Kala being a reasonable woman, did not follow the rules of the caste system. She was the first Brahmin lady in the town to have a non-Brahmin maid in the house. She had raised her children that way too. Mithila never did understand for years, why some of her friends never ate at her house or offered her food at theirs. As an adult, Mithila grew to respect her mother immensely for her modern outlook in that day and age.

Adhira mixed the rice, curry and vegetable in a pot and served the food. The image of Kala eating every morsel with tears streaming down her face would stay ingrained in the memory of all those who witnessed it, for the rest of their lives.

★ ★ ★

The Agony Of Eviction

The television volume was louder than normal. *Thata* (grandfather in Tamil) was hard of hearing since a few months. Chitra was sitting on the wide wooden swing eating her lunch of yoghurt and rice with mango pickle. She and thata were watching the weekend movie on television. This was a routine. The movie was getting more melodramatic by the minute. The scene changed to where the protagonist's mother and sister were thrown out of their house because they had lost the house, unable to pay back the money they borrowed. Chitra stood up to go to the kitchen to put back her plate. She noticed her thata's face was streaming with tears. She had seldom known her grandpa to cry. Upset, she ran to her mother, who was standing by the shelf tidying things.

"Amma, thata is crying..."

To her surprise, her mother's eyes too filled with tears, which now were falling down her cheeks. Lost for words, Chitra stood confused in her tracks. She wondered what was so emotional about this movie. Did she miss something?

"Mithila, the water is boiling for a long time now. Turn off the flame!"

Mithila quickly wiped her tears on hearing her husband's voice, took her daughter's plate and went back to the kitchen.

It would be ten more years before Chitra learned the tale behind her mother's tears. She would never find the reason behind her grandfather's.

THE TEACHER

"Kala *chechi*, Kala chechi! Shiva *cheta* is at it again!" A neighbour shouted a warning from the gate.

Kala was hanging out clothes in the courtyard while three of her children played in the house and the fourth one sat near the bucket of clothes. She hit her hand on her forehead in exasperation, she lifted the infant Balachandran onto her waist and held him with one hand, and rushed to the gate.

"What has he been up to now? Never will I have a minute's peace in this life with this man!"

The village of Muvattupuzha was situated on the banks of the river of the same name. A beautiful quaint village, it was ridden with the grime of politics though. The village was also famed for its high levels of literacy. There was a constant demand for school teachers in the two government schools. One school was for the boys and the smaller one situated a few km away was for the girls.

Shiva had passed the teachers' training course with the highest marks in the state that year. His score and his mastery of British English opened many doors for him and he had job offers from across the state.

The Teacher

He decided to take up a job as a teacher here in his native village. Kala was not too pleased having to now stay with her in-laws and it would not be unfair to say that they were quite unpleasant to her.

While the authorities would have preferred hiring female teachers for the girls' school, they were hard to find. Kerala had the earliest girls' school established in the 19th century. But it did take time for girls' schools to spring up in the entire state. The drop-out rates were still high a century later. In this village, women had only recently started to attend schools. This generation would produce the first female graduates of soon-to-be independent India!

Shiva found himself as the teacher of the girls' school and was handed the responsibility of teaching Mathematics, English, Malayalam, and Social Studies for Stds I to VII. The school was not equipped for higher classes. As the girls progressed the grades were added along.

Kala was partial to her sons, one may blame it on the patterns and ideologies of those days. But Shiva loved his daughters more than anything in the world. He was not a traditional father, nor was he a responsible family man. He was utterly delighted to have the opportunity to teach girls. Shiva was a man trapped in the twilight zone with modern ideologies way ahead of his times whilst adhering to raising his children with classic patriarchal ideologies of his times. He was an enigma, even to those closest to him.

In a few months, Shiva was well settled into his role as a teacher. He shuffled classes with four other teachers. Due to the scarcity of teachers, they would often club adjacent classes into one. Hence classes would often have students of varying ages. There were quite a few older girls in the younger batches too, having entered school in their later years.

One Thursday morning, Shiva was explaining the mathematical equation for velocity. He cited a few examples.

"Have you seen a man run and have you seen a bullock cart in motion? Which is faster?"

"The cart!", "My father", and "My bullock is so lazy!" came in multiple answers across the room causing much mirth.

Shiva reframed the question. "Is a car faster than a running man?"

The class was silent. Shiva realised the children had never seen a car in their tiny village.

"Well, let's put it this way. Is a man swimming in our river faster than a boat being rowed upon it?"

Shiva beamed at having found a wonderful example that they may have experienced daily.

"The boat, teacher!"

"Excellent yes! That is the right answer. Why is the boat faster? Can you tell me?"

The Teacher

The class didn't have an answer.

"Do not be afraid. What do you think is the reason? Vaidehi, Anasuya, how does the boatman row?"

The girls sat mute looking confused. "Show me the action of rowing. You have seen it, haven't you?"

The girls nodded their heads indicating no.

Shiva questioned the class, "Who can show me how the boatman rows? In what direction? What do his oars do to push the boat ahead?"

Kantha in the first row answered, "Teacher, we have not been on a boat."

"What! You have lived all your life in a village by the river and have never been on a boat? How ridiculous is this!"

Shiva thought for a minute, but he could not go on with his lesson. He told the batch of 12 teenagers, "Get up and follow me."

The confused girls got up and reluctantly did as he commanded.

Shiva followed by the shy girls, walked out of the school gates, through the fields, lanes, and marketplace before reaching the riverbank where the boatmen waited.

It was not a daily sight to witness for the humble villagers. The girls were seldom outdoors beyond their school hours and the walk from home to school and back. On the rare occasion when they did venture outdoors, it would be with family members including their parents, elder brothers and the like. Some of the over-protected girls were embarrassed at being outside. The marketplace especially went into a tizzy seeing the girls following a man like Pied Piper.

"*Vaadiyar* (teacher), where are you taking these girls?"

"*Swami* (a respectful term for a learned Tamil Brahmin man), where are you off to?"

"Shiva, what is going on?"

Shiva ignored everyone. He was a man on a mission.

The boatmen didn't dare refuse Shiva as he asked two of them to accommodate the girls in each boat. Shiva joined one and off they went on a ride to the other bank.

The weather was beautiful that afternoon. The afternoon sunrays reached the bottom of the grey-white clean river near the riverbanks. The skies felt generous and the breeze ensured the temperature was not too hot. The gurgling of the strong river mingled with the delightful giggles of the young girls. Oh, what a wonderful memory this was to become for these children for life!

As they hit the other bank, Shiva asked the boatmen to take them back.

The Teacher

He paid the boatmen generously and marched the now boisterous group of girls back to school.

Once within the school gates, the school principal was found waiting for them.

"Shiva, where did you disappear with the students?"

Shiva replied with nonchalance, "Teaching them velocity!"

He walked back into class, to continue his lesson on velocity.

Unbeknownst to what awaited him after this day at home, in the neighbourhood and in the principal's office.

Little did Shiva realise, that the boat ride on that particular day would remain the only fun outing some of the girls would ever experience in their entire restricted lives.

A week passed. Shiva was transferred to the boys' school. He continued his job as before, though he did miss the disciplined female students of the past. But nothing much changed in his life. The students in the girls' school though ended up losing the only radical teacher they would ever have in their lifetime.

A HOME TO REMEMBER

Those kind eyes he spent the last few minutes looking at, smiled back at him sweetly. How beautiful and graceful and dignified she was! Despite her short and diminutive nature, her strong will and strength were obvious to all who knew her. Krishna closed his wallet in which he carried his dear mother's photograph and placed it in his pocket. He was alert but not anxious. His stomach growled, reminding him that it had been more than 48 hours since he had last eaten. He wiped the sweat from his palms on his pants but was glad that his hands were still as steady as a rock. He looked out of the window at the waves forming in the Arabian Sea which seemed to be calm that day. Considering it would be his first interview, it was an achievement in itself. He had applied at the law firm called Manilal Mehta & Giridhar Rao for the position of clerk.

Krishna's parents, Manohari Raghava and Veera Krishna Iyer were wed in the small town of Perumbavoor in the Ernakulam district. The bride and groom saw each other for the first time on the day of their wedding; a fleeting glance, since for the rest of the ceremony the groom kept his eyes fixed on the

A Home To Remember

ceremonial fire and the teenage bride gazed at the floor. A difference of 15 years between them did not raise any eyebrows as it was quite common in that generation. In the forthcoming years, she would skilfully manage the heavy housework in her husband's spacious home and raise 12 children.

Krishna, the eldest of the siblings, named after his grandfather, could vividly remember every nook and corner of his lovely home. Large spacious rooms, high ceilings, strong dark-coloured artistic pillars supporting the sloping roof, the central sky-lit area that welcomed the rain and the sun alike, the plinth in the front where many conversations took place over steaming cups of filter *kaapi*. The jackfruit and banana trees, the cashew trees, the mangrove laden with ripe fruits, which would fall with a strong mid-afternoon gust of wind, which would send the children in the neighbourhood running to see who gathers the maximum fruits, the tall coconut trees that gracefully danced during storms, playing against the moonlight on these dreadful stormy nights, the humble *tulsi* (basil) plant his mother watered religiously every morning invoking the blessings of the goddess before the day began. How he missed the warmth of home, the coconut-rich curries and par-boiled rice, the dense greenery, the warm musical lilt of the local language, Malayalam, and his father calling out to him and giving orders in Tamil and switching over to British English when angry, his siblings running to him for every small matter. His father and his forefathers before him were landowners and bankers. They were comfortable and food was available in abundance, thanks to the fertile soil of Kerala. Theirs was a household of devout Brahmins, who were pure vegetarians by religion as well as by principle.

Brilliant, responsible, disciplined and armed with a fierce temper, Krishna was looked upon with great regard by his siblings, friends, neighbours and even his teachers. He was always at the top of his class. He was a state topper in the final school year board exams. Being the firstborn, he was the apple of his mother's eye. Her wish was his command. But his mother was never the demanding kind. Unlike the fear and discipline his father inspired, the children found their mother more accessible to bring their woes and troubles. His mother, Manohari was a gentle soft-spoken soul. Maintaining the huge house without any help, her constant state of being either pregnant or nursing, took a toll on her already fragile health. She suffered a respiratory ailment for years before she finally succumbed to it when Krishna was 20 years old. Suddenly the patriarch of the house was faced with the responsibility of raising a dozen children between the ages of 1.5 and 18 years. Whenever he faltered the elder children took charge. So, Krishna was like a parent more than a brother to his younger siblings.

Krishna was drafted into the Indian army at a very young age. He was posted in a remote village in Karnataka when the fateful telegram arrived. At that time, he had a high fever and chills caused by chicken pox. He read the telegram: "Amma is no more. Come home earliest."

At once, the world he knew came crashing down. It would now forever be a world devoid of the warmth and love of his beloved Amma.

Krishna packed his few belongings and travelled the long distance to his village in Kerala by train with what little energy he had left. In those days, those suffering from skin rash and vesicles were not allowed on trains. In an age where the final fight against smallpox was in order, laymen did not differentiate between smallpox and other lesser virulent exanthems. Krishna had to hide under the seat of the lowest berth. He spent the entire journey tucked under the seat without anything to eat or drink, hidden from the ticket collectors and officials. His fever had sky-rocketed. His body was quaking at a greater frequency than the reverberations of the train. In a half-delirious state, he arrived at his destination taking twice the time due to delays.

At home, the sight that welcomed him seemed worse than his sickness. The entire neighbourhood had gathered in front of his house, the one his family had owned for generations. Gloom and despair were palpable in the atmosphere. His father was sitting at the threshold of his home with his face bent down and his hand against his forehead, the posture of a man, who could no longer put up a fight and was defeated

Stories My Grandma Never Told Me

by the troubles of life. His gaze was answered by a look of a man who had lost purpose and meaning in life. He walked past his father, still very weak from his illness and entered his home. The house had a central courtyard that opened to the sky. The front room was wide and spacious with a high ceiling. This room was where all celebrations and festivities had taken place. A room full of life, love and laughter, even during the dark days of political instability and poverty. His 11 siblings sat scattered in the hall. The younger ones were crying in the arms of the older children. The older ones now struggled to keep control of their emotions. On seeing their eldest brother, everyone broke down and ran to be held in their brother's arms to cry and relieve themselves of the profound pain and sense of loss that only one who has lost his mother can feel and comprehend. His eyes now scanned the room and fell upon the most prominent feature. His mother's body draped in white, was laid across the centre of the hall, and decked in flowers. At the head, a lamp was lit. A white sheet covered her exposing only her head and her feet. The big toes of both feet were tied together with a string. As per custom, the body was kept in the north-south direction and a garland of marigolds adorned the neck and torso. Krishna could almost hear her voice scolding him once when he lay on his bed in the same direction, "Krishna, place your head on the pillow and sleep right!" Sleeping in the east-west direction is considered optimal as per Indian traditional science.

A Home To Remember

Your body is believed to be in sync with the earth's magnetic field when you lie perpendicular to it.

As the eldest son, it was his duty to perform the death rites of his mother. Being a Brahmin household, the rites were detailed and spanned over 13 days.

After a few hours, they walked to the cremation grounds carrying the body. Pouring cold water over himself, shivering and breaking down each time he uttered a mantra, he realised he was bidding a final farewell to his mother. The funeral pyre was lit. Slowly the crowd began to dwindle. Krishna stood there the entire night watching it burn. It was his final farewell.

The sense of loss upon his mother's death was ever-present in Krishna's life. The pain was subtly palpable even in his most joyous moments. Today was no exception. He looked at his mother's black and white photograph for a long time. It had been taken a few days after her 29th birthday. Her serene smile and calm face gazed back at him lovingly. They had prepared a traditional feast at home with the classic south Indian style rice pudding (*payasam*), enriched with nuts roasted in clarified butter. She was so happy on that day. Seldom had one heard her laugh so loud. Ah... That now seemed like a long time ago. He could only see that face in the photo of hers secure in his wallet and in the infinite memories of the hand that rocked his cradle, the hand he held as he took his first step, the face that calmed him in the stormiest night, the lovely voice that sang Carnatic music songs to make him sleep instead of mundane lullabies.

Time dulled the pain. The responsibility to nurture and feed his father and siblings took precedence. Not everyone had the luxury to grieve for a prolonged period. Krishna worked to find his footing in this world with many odd jobs, sending home his salary in envelopes along with letters for his father.

A few years later, Krishna found himself in a new city. He hoped for new opportunities here. He sat in nervous anticipation in the waiting room of the firm for his job interview. The brown door opened halfway. A tense, nervous man rushed out; his white shirt half soaked in sweat and sped out of the hall. A man in a black jacket followed.

"Krishna Iyer! Please come in."

Half an hour later, the door reopened. The man who walked out of that room strode out of the building like one who had won a war, in the city that had recently become his home. A man with a razor-sharp intellect, two hands willing to work as hard as it would take, and a will as strong as the ancient mountains.

Krishna crossed the street to face the sea. The humid, salty, sea breeze grew stronger. He felt at home. He smiled and closed his eyes. He knew Mumbai had him in her embrace now. And she would never let go.

PARLE G

Adhira began to unpack the bags her father-in-law Krishna Iyer brought home. She brought out the largest steel and aluminium jars from the store room. A stack of books, magazines, and comics lay strewn in the living room. Her young brother-in-law sat in one corner with a few friends poring over Phantom, Mandrake, Chandamama, Amar Chitra Katha and Tinkle comics. A neighbour sat in another corner sorting out the vegetables Krishna had purchased, hoping to take back a share for her kitchen later. Adhira opened the other bags and started to stock up the potato wafers, banana chips, *chivda*, *chakli*, peanuts, assorted nuts, and others. The third jar was to be filled with biscuits of every kind. She started to put away the packets one by one. Marie, Good Day, Top, Nice, Monaco, Jim Jam, an array of cream biscuits and cheeslings. The last was a huge packet of Parle G biscuits. As she was mechanically doing the chore, this packet made her stop and the floodgates of nostalgia opened.

Everything disappeared. She was five years old once again, in Ernakulam, Kerala. For reasons her young mind could not fathom, her family had to keep moving houses. That particular year they were sharing

Stories My Grandma Never Told Me

a tiny house with another family. She would visit her rich uncle's house once every month for prayer and Carnatic music meets. Adhira was conscious of her sullied old clothes as her rich cousins swayed in their silk *pavadais* (full-length skirts, usually of silk with a gold-rimmed border) and gold chains and bangles. She never longed for any of these. But, she wished they would treat her like a sibling rather than like a maid's child. Her mother Kala was not treated well in that house being the wife of a poor man.

During one of these meetings, her uncle gave each of her bratty rich cousins and their friends a packet of Parle-G biscuits. While she sat at the end of the room hiding behind her mother, they shared the packets between themselves, knowing full well that a hungry five-year-old's eyes were on them. Her mother noticed this and reduced visits to her brother's place after this episode. She couldn't bear to see the hurt in her child's eyes.

Adhira grew up to have simple wants in life. She was happy with three saris, and a pair of repaired footwear for college. At times, it seemed her parents did not quite appreciate what an undemanding child she was. She was happy with the 'precious' stones she discovered in the pristine sands of Kerala. She would collect flowers along the way from school and make jewellery by threading them in varied patterns. One time her eldest brother unexpectedly gave her a few coins. She bought beads from the market with those. For the next few months, every week she would make a different patterned necklace with those beads. Her friends would eagerly wait at the start of each week to see what Adhira had created. One sad day, during a fight between her parents, her mother threw out a lot of items. That particular day Adhira had left behind her bead jewellery in the rush to get to school. She never did see them again.

The next time she had jewellery would be for her wedding. Her parents and in particular her elder brothers had gathered the little money they had to ensure the bride had two beautiful gold chains and earrings. The groom's side had demanded very little dowry. Her father-in-law Krishna was a self-respecting, self-made man.

"Mr Shiva, I have enough money to feed my own and many more by God's grace. I don't need your money. Nor do I seek any gifts. All I know is that I seek to have Adhira as a bride for my eldest son Subramanian."

Her father Shiva was very impressed by Krishna's outlook and agreed to the match at the very first meeting, without even having met the groom or taken Adhira's consent for the marriage. Her parents were thankful and excited that their little one would now be part of a wealthy family and never sleep hungry. As for Adhira, all she dreamed of was completing her graduation and working. Alas, that was not meant to be. She had no choice in this matter. Her mother had her hands full with her younger siblings and her sisters-in-law were not keen on having her around. She confided in her friend on the day of the wedding, "I feel like a lamb being led to slaughter." Her friend bawled her eyes out.

Recently married and forced to quit college, she learned to manage her new house early on. Not a woman of many words, she worked all day long. A new city, a new family, a new last name, and some broken dreams of education and a job. She blocked the thoughts by going through her daily chores and cleaning. The past lay buried. The pain ignored. The future unknown.

'A poor man's daughter doesn't have choices in life,' she reminded herself now and then, accepting her fate and continuing to cook multiple meals every day for a dozen people or more.

But there was this unfulfilled wish from childhood that stayed pending or rather buried in her – to eat an entire pack of Parle-G biscuits without sharing it with anyone. Yes. Surprisingly, that was her only wish from childhood to her late teens. She had forgotten about this.

But today, her entire childhood flashed through her mind when she lay eyes on that packet of Parle G. It was her and the biscuit alone. She opened the packet, took one and bit into it. The sweetness sank into her bringing with it all the bitterness of days bygone. She finished the biscuit and dipped her hands again to take another one. Before she knew it, she had finished one packet. There were nine more packets in the box.

"Adhira, *enna idu* (what's this)? Why are you still sitting instead of packing away all this?" Came a voice from the doorway. Adhira quickly returned to her senses and took the jars away to the store room one by one. The tears streaming down her face went unnoticed. Tears of a bygone hard past, of dreams she had given up, of feeling unloved, and most of all of the realisation that this packet of Parle G had come too late, much after its magic had worn off, one that would never now satiate the hunger of that child from 20 years ago.

THE MUSICIAN AND HIS MUSE

The milkman sang hoarsely, "*Dil deewana, bin sajana ke, maane naaaa…*" He knocked on the door to match the beats of the tune.

'Always the same song. Always!' murmured Mukundan as he struggled to fight lethargy, getting up from his bed, putting his feet on the ground and dragging himself to the kitchen. He brought a vessel and opened the door with a big yawn. "*Bhaiya, adha* litre, (Brother, half a litre)" he said ordering the milk.

"Lala..la.. la..la.. na na..na.aaa…aaaa…" the milkman now focused on the purity of the melody. Having poured the milk, he walked next door, with a spring in his step.

'Crazy chap!' said Mukundan to himself. 'How does he stay so energetic and happy so early in the day? Phew!'

He placed the vessel on the stove and rubbed his mop of luxuriant hair. He hated mornings. As the milk was about to boil over, he turned off the stove and went to make himself a cup of coffee. He shook his head in disappointment as he picked up the packet of instant coffee. He missed the filter *kaapi* of Bangalore.

The Musician And His Muse

Having grown up in a house where coffee would flow abundantly, he regretted that he had never learnt to prepare filter coffee. He was now trying to make peace with the instant one. He took the cup of coffee and the two Parle-G biscuits to the balcony. The biscuits and the coffee were habits he had picked up from his mother. Not a hint of the slightest breeze. Summers in Mumbai were unforgiving. Of all the months that he could have chosen to move here, it had to be mid-May!

The phone rang. He walked back inside knowing full well who the caller was.

"Mukundan, *eppudi irrukai* (how are you)? How is the new place?"

Mukundan smiled widely hearing his mother's voice. "Amma, I miss your coffee so much!"

Adhira laughed but her son could sense the sadness she felt being away from him. She called him twice a day.

He finished the coffee and biscuits during his conversation with her.

He didn't quite like his tiny room and the area initially but it had grown on him over the past few weeks. Bangalore certainly had a different vibe, but Mumbai had a charm that was hard to explain. He recollected his friend's words about Mumbai, "She is hard to love when you have just met her. But once you get to know her even a little, she will grip you with a force and an intensity you never would expect, and then it's forever! There is no going back. And even if you leave, you will never again fall in love as passionately with any other city! Never!"

Mukundan had ridiculed the idea when he first heard of it. But now he felt a stirring in his soul. The dusty, packed roads, the cacophony of the marketplace, the straightforward – to the point of being positively rude – locals, the relentlessness and survival strength of those who call this city home, the festivity during religious holidays, he was slowly but surely falling in love, with this vibrant city. He now found beauty even in the mundane and the ugliness of the city.

The thriving three-storeyed *chawl* (tenement) opposite had so many stories to tell. So did the flower girl, the rickshaw puller, the clock repair guy, the rag-picker, the officer goer, the super-efficient *dabba* (lunchbox) delivery professionals, and the rich industrialist stuck in his car at the traffic signal. Mumbai belonged to everyone.

He exchanged the cup for his flute and walked to the balcony.

It was three weeks since he got here. He had stayed with a friend for this period and later found himself this place and moved in five days ago. While the area was noisy and crowded, it was easy to travel to the office from here and the rent was cheaper.

The Musician And His Muse

He lifted the flute elegantly to his dry chapped lips and played the tune that first came into his head. "*Dil deewana...bin sajana ke...*", he stopped immediately and chuckled. Damn that milkman for giving him an earworm!

This flute was very precious to him. It was gifted to him by his maternal grandmother. Kala *paati* (grandmother in Tamil) was the one who had insisted that Mukundan be enrolled for music lessons as a child. No matter how many flutes he had played with, he always received the most resounding praise when he played with the one Kala gave.

He stopped playing the flute for a while and let the sights and sounds from across and below the balcony sink in for inspiration. While everything was pretty much what he had witnessed these mornings, his attention was captured by a lady wearing a bright orange sari, her hair caught up in a high tight bun. She was holding a glass of tea in her left hand and bent over ever so slightly on the railing of the wide balcony spanning across the second floor of the chawl opposite him. The colour of her sari was the same as the flag of a local political party. He kept staring at her. In all the chaos, impatience, honking and abuses of a typical morning in this area, she was a picture of calm. She had all the time in the world. An eternity seemed to pass between two sips of her tea. He felt time slowing down as he studied this mysterious creature.

Suddenly she looked straight at him. Caught off guard, he felt embarrassed, but soon recovered and smiled and waved at her. His friendliness was returned with a stoic gaze. He looked away and started playing the flute again with his eyes closed. He was in a different zone now. A magical land where everything else ceased to exist and the music flowed. He played Raag Malhar and tunes based on this *raga* for what must have been 20 minutes or more. He opened his eyes, a different man. His breathing was calmer, his heart rate slower, and was feeling refreshed, almost enlightened. He was about to turn and walk indoors when a smile from the chawl across the street caused him to stop mid-turn. The smile belonged to the lady in the orange sari. She nodded in approval and did a *hamsasya mudra* (index finger and thumb touching at the tips while the other three fingers are raised.)

Mukundan smiled gratefully, bowed his head and walked in.

This became a daily routine. He would speak to his mother on the phone, have his coffee, then take his flute to play on the balcony while his new-found melophile friend would eagerly be waiting with her glass of tea.

When he finished playing a piece, he would look straight at her for an immediate verdict. She would do a thumbs up if it was 'Good', hamsasya mudra meant 'Excellent', horizontally placed hand with all fingers stretched with a fast seesaw motion meant 'Okay-ish', while a thumbs down meant 'Don't play this again' or 'Go practice!'

He started to make a mental note of what she liked and what she didn't. She had an unusual choice of music. It was hard to predict what she would like, he realised. She did seem to like Raag Malhar, Raag Hamsadhwani, a lot of Dev Anand, Waheeda Rehman era songs and Shah Rukh Khan movie songs of recent days. That's all he had come to conclude so far. He once played a Sufi song and she clapped! Another time he played a folk song and he got a thumbs down. Surprisingly the day he played Raag Bhairavi after having practised for days in his room, she broke his heart with disapproval. Women are said to be moody and unpredictable rightly, he consoled himself.

Mornings no longer seemed a drag for Mukundan. Rather he found himself waking up early to finish his coffee, comb his hair and wash his face before he went out to the balcony to play music.

Three months of pleasurable mornings later, she disappeared. One fine morning she was not there. Mukundan hesitantly turned back to his room. He was in no mood to play his flute. On the fourth day, to his utter delight, she appeared again! In a departure from her usual bright-coloured sari, she was wearing a cotton nightgown. She looked pale, and tired, her dishevelled long hair in a loose ponytail. She seemed to have lost weight in this short duration. He waved eagerly as she smiled. She held her usual glass of tea in her hand. He raised his hand, palm outwards to touch his forehead, then brought his hand down in the *alapadma mudra* (fingers spread in a flower-like pattern- indicates a question in a non-dance world). She nodded, and repeated the forehead gesture with her palm, indicating fever and illness. He smiled in compassion, glad that she was on the road to recovery. He ran in and got out the flute he hadn't played for the few days she had not come out. Her face brightened as he started to weave music out of thin air.

She soon recovered and was back to her bright pink, yellow, orange, and blue saris. Their communication using gestures had now improved to the next level. They could converse for minutes together and even crack jokes. They started spending those rare free evenings together across their respective balconies. He witnessed the Ganesh Chaturthi processions with her opposite him in glee. For Diwali, they both lit *diyas* (oil lamps) in their windows and balconies at the same time, and he wore an orange kurta, which she seemed to love.

Mukundan's playing improved with this regular practice and feedback. He worked from late morning till late evening. His life was a drag with corporate pressures. With time, as the workload increased, he found that this morning ritual of music, coffee and conversation was the only thing that brought joy and sanity to his otherwise lonely life.

A year passed by. One day, she held out a glass of tea in her right hand, and he saw her left arm hanging from a sling with a fresh white plaster cast on her left arm. He was worried. She laughed and in action, explained how she fell forward while she was walking and injured her arm. In six weeks, the cast was out, and she danced with her arms in the air the next morning.

One winter morning, he played the flute as usual and then conveyed to her that he was travelling for the next seven days. He lifted and moved his hand high across the sky to indicate a plane, and showed seven fingers. She reacted to the information with a thumbs up.

The day Mukundan returned; he found her balcony empty. The next morning, instead of the milkman's hoarse singing, he woke up to the ambulance siren. He ran to the balcony. There were two police vans in the street and the ambulance had just arrived. A lot of people had gathered at the entrance of the opposite chawl. He looked up to see two constables walking to the second-level balcony. She was nowhere to be seen. He noticed a third police constable leave her house. Mukundan ran out of his house and towards the crowd below her chawl.

The police prevented anyone from entering. A lady constable and a paramedic soon emerged, assisting the young woman between them. The young lady's pink sari had streaks of red. Her nose and mouth were bleeding, her eyelid was swollen. While she could walk with help, she did have a limp and was bleeding profusely. They laid her on the stretcher and the sirens came on again as the ambulance flew into the main street. Mukundan was in shock as he watched his friend being taken away. As the crowds began to disperse along, he went up to a middle-aged lady who was about to enter the chawl and asked her what had happened.

"*Kay sangaycha ata*? (What is there to say anymore?) This is not something new. Her husband keeps hitting her every day. Some days are so bad, but well, never has it been as terrible as today."

Few more women joined in.

"Do you remember she had a miscarriage after he pushed her down the stairs last year? She lost so much blood and was pale as a ghost. *Bechari* (poor thing). Can't speak or hear as it is, and to top that an abusive husband!"

"I told her parents to file a police complaint when she got that fracture. Men like Keshav don't deserve to be treated as humans!"

"Her folks won't do anything. They just wanted to get her married. I am glad he has been put in jail! Won't be easy to get out. Dowry demands and torture of a mute and hearing-impaired person are serious crimes. Hopefully, she recovers soon. She will likely be free of her evil husband after this!"

The Musician And His Muse

Mukundan was numb with pain and shock. He walked back to his room in a daze. The next few weeks, he found her balcony empty. As empty as his soul felt. Bereft of joy, of music.

Three months later, he found someone standing on the same balcony opposite him. He ran out. This lady wore a flowing white *kurta* and her shoulder-length hair was worn loose, some strands falling on her dusky face. He couldn't see her face. She disappeared into his friend's house and returned with a glass of tea in her left hand. She looked straight at him and smiled. Aah! That beautiful, beautiful smile. The smile that charmed his mornings until the recent past, how could he not recognise that? He grinned from ear to ear, and his heart soared to see her. They laughed for a long while in unbridled joy. He questioned her, pointing at her house and donning an imaginary garland on his neck and an open hand gesture *(alapadma)* asking "Where?" She tilted her head to throw back a stray hair, and moved her open hand horizontally across her neck in a slicing manner, rolling her eyes up and pulling out her tongue and tilting her head back and sideways. They both laughed heartily!

She gestured playing an imaginary flute. He ran inside to get the flute that had gathered dust on the shelf over the last few months. Today he would play the best music of his life!

A music piece dedicated to his friend from across the street. Separated by a few metres and plenty of commotion, a friendship whose boundaries lay within those two balconies, but whose bounds encompassed two human lives; joy and music shared across time. He played a starkly beautiful and haunting melody, that rose from the core of his very being, the first and last of his compositions; the lyrics of which were her smile, her strength and purity. A melody that she would and could never hear.

Or, could she hear the music from this particular flute? Did not Adhira say some in the neighbourhood thought that Kala was a sorceress? Mukundan wondered if all that she ever could hear in this noisy world were the notes of his music alone.

She nodded her head eagerly after he finished playing and clapped in great excitement. He grinned and bowed his head. He had another secret that he would never let her know.

He now knew her name.

Vaani.*

---

* **Vaani** – means speech in Sanskrit

THE TEEN BRIDE

It was an unforgettable night.

A night without emancipation.

"She fell in, as she was drawing water from the well."

Shantipriya looked with disbelief at her mother-in-law.

Parmeshwaran had a fiery temper, infamous across the village and the neighbouring ones too. His father had a nightmarish time finding him a bride. His elder son had been married for three years already. He was getting desperate to find a bride for the younger one.

Ambujam's father was a cook. Parmeshwaran came across him at a wedding he attended in Kanyakumari. A poor man, he was overwhelmed with the proposal. The groom's family did not demand extravagant dowry either.

Ambujam saw her soon-to-be husband in the wedding hall for the first time.

She was a quiet, simple girl who had grown up without a mother and was raised in poverty by her father. He used to cook for Iyer (Tamil Brahmin) weddings and functions. At times, he travelled from village to village, leaving his children in the care of his mother. His mother was a cruel woman, a product of her circumstances. She never did let her granddaughters take a minute's rest. Ambujam took charge of the cooking when she was barely seven years old.

She was a bright girl but was not allowed to go to school. The girls' school saw little if any attendance at all in their village. Yet the social workers kept visiting the houses sure of a change in the future.

Barely 16, Ambujam packed her bags to head off to her husband's family, not knowing that it would be the last time she would see her grandmother.

It was not an easy task adjusting to her husband and his orthodox family. But she did like Perumbavoor. The village houses were big and spacious, the courtyards laden with plenty of jackfruits, mango, coconut trees and many root vegetables. The hibiscus plants were laden with multicoloured flowers all through the year. Ambujam would wake up before dawn, have a bath in the cold pond near their house, visit the Lord Shiva temple and then tend to her kitchen and house duties. The housework was tiring but her mother-in-law helped her a little with the cooking. She didn't mind the scolding much. Derision and denigration were the staples for daughters-in-law.

In the afternoon she would get two hours to herself. She loved taking a short nap and then she would go for

The Teen Bride

a walk in the afternoon sun in the courtyard. In the evening, her husband would return home. It was not hard to predict what his mood would be like. He was always angry and screaming.

Parmeshwaran and his family ran a money-lending business. His foul moods hence were aplenty.

Eight months into the marriage Ambujam missed her period. There was great joy in the family. They awaited a few more months before announcing the news to their relatives. The joyful news though didn't translate into easing up the pregnant woman's house duties.

"Work more now. That is how the child will be healthy and you will have an easier labour," advised her mother-in-law as the four-month-pregnant woman sat on a small wooden stool for hours together with a large stone grinder in front of her, using all her strength to churn the *dosa* batter (rice and lentil pancake batter) with the boulder in a circular motion and wiping the sweat off her forehead and neck with a towel intermittently.

After dusk, Parmeshwaran and his brother returned home and had their dinner. Ambujam cleaned up and served her mother-in-law and sister-in-law dinner following which she ate what little was left. Parmeshwaran and his brother would sit on the large wooden swing in the centre hall discussing matters of the day while their wives would stand near them and prepare a pack of betel leaf coated with lime and betel nut for them. This particular day was exceptionally exhausting.

Ambujam wondered if all this manual labour would aid her in birthing the child. She often prayed to Lord Shiva, that she never wished to be reborn as a girl. It was not an easy life for a woman. She cleaned the kitchen and washed the vessels. Today they had a few unexpected guests in the afternoon. There was barely any food for her. The growing child in her made her feel famished all day and night.

She opened the back door of the kitchen to walk out in the cool air of the courtyard.

Parmeshwaran was seated on the swing with his brother. His sister-in-law, Shantipriya served her husband the customary betel leaf and went off to bed. He waited for a few minutes for his wife to serve him. Not finding her, he called out a few times. He heard no response.

His brother laughed mockingly. Parmeshwaran was livid and stormed into the kitchen. He found the backdoor open. Ambujam was walking in the courtyard taking slow steps, staring up at the moon.

"Ambujam, what in the world are you doing here? Who is to give me my betel leaf? Should I get myself another wife to make up for the lousy one that you are?"

The poor young girl was terrified and dumbstruck. She stood transfixed.

"Don't just stand there, useless creature! I regret doing my father a favour by agreeing to marry you."

He walked up to her and held her long braid at the nape of her neck and dragged her inside the house to the hall. He released her hair and pushed her in front of the swing. His brother laughed in appreciation as the pregnant woman fell on the floor.

"You make me hit you every day with your irresponsible behaviour. I return tired after work only to find I have to discipline my stupid wife!"

Ambujam was embarrassed as her sari pallu gave way and at being so callously and cruelly flung on the ground, in front of her brother-in-law.

She hastily wiped her pouring tears, ignored the searing pain in her scalp, set her sari right to cover herself, stood up and rushed to walk towards her bedroom.

Parmeshwaran held her wrist and pulled her back.

"This will not do. You will never learn if I let go easily."

He slapped her multiple times; she fell to the ground with each slap. Her cheeks were flaming red and searing in pain. He asked her to get up each time she fell.

After a few minutes, she was in extreme trauma and stayed on the floor.

Her head felt dizzy, and she felt faint with pain and hurt. The thought of bringing up a child with this man and God forbid if this was a daughter, imagining her daughter going through the same pain, hurt her far more deeply than these verbal insults and physical wounds.

She thought of her father. The warm days of childhood when she didn't have anything to call her own in terms of material possessions, yet she was so happy running through the rice fields, and playing with her friends.

She stayed in this memory. It made the torture bearable.

Parmeshwaran flew into a fit of rage when she stayed on the floor, and disobeyed his command of "Get up you lazy pig!"

He turned her over with a flick of his leg and kicked her hard a second time on her stomach.

A shriek could be heard in the entire household that terrorized the very core of all under the roof.

Shantipriya and his mother came running in. His father was deaf and continued his slumber oblivious to the violence.

Ambujam lay curled up on the floor like an infant and there was blood emanating from her sari.

The Teen Bride

The blood looked bright red against the maroon floor. The women rushed by the injured woman's side.

Ambujam's face was red, drenched in sweat, and her breathing was shallow and rapid. They tried in vain to calm her and the blood to their horror covered much of the floor as each minute passed.

Her face turned pale in another ten minutes. Shantipriya felt her pulse. She felt a weak pulse and that was a sure sign of impending doom.

Ambujam breathed her last, taking with her the child conceived inside her.

The silence that followed as realisation hit the household, spoke of a sinister night.

A night of no emancipation.

Worse was to come.

"Call the *Vaidyan* (doctor)!" Screamed Shantipriya holding Ambujam's cold clammy body.

Her mother-in-law interrupted her. "Nobody is going anywhere, nor are we calling anyone. She is dead."

She paced the hall for a long time. She looked at her elder son's face and they read each other's mind.

"Shanta, take Parmeshwaran to his room and let him try to sleep. You lock yourself up with the children. We will deal with this."

Stories My Grandma Never Told Me

Shanta was confused and in shock but obeyed her dominating mother-in-law.

Ambujam was wrapped in a sheet to prevent blood from dripping across. She was unceremoniously carried by her brother-in-law to the kitchen and out to the backyard, as her mother-in-law opened the doors. She was flung into the well. The thud could be heard after three seconds.

Two weeks later Krishna Iyer visited the family.

"*Anna* (brother), I heard what happened to *Manni* (a respectful term for sister-in-law in Tamil). So tragic and unfair! She was so young and was she not expecting a child?" asked Krishna, Parameshwaran's cousin, who was particularly fond of Ambujam.

Krishna was visibly shattered. He respected his sister-in-law Ambujam a lot and she was all ears for stories of his army days. Krishna was never particularly close to his cousin Parmeshwaran but looked forward to meeting him and his wife at family events because of his fondness for Ambujam. Onlookers often mistook them for siblings. Such was their camaraderie.

Krishna spent a few hours with his cousin. As he was leaving, he took a detour to the back and bent over the sinister well. He failed to hear the wails of the tormented soul of his sister-in-law and her unborn child.

Six months later Krishna received a wedding invitation.

'You are graciously invited to attend the wedding ceremony of Parmeshwaran and Seethalakshmi'.

THE FIRST-BORN

It was a girl.

The entire neighbourhood could hear Kala's wails through the night. Kala grieved for a lost soul, for what would have been her youngest. She breathed for 23 minutes. Her little body and lungs could not hold on any longer. She was born two months premature.

The next day, Kala wore a white blouse with her deep red nine-yard sari. For the rest of her life, she only wore white blouses with her saris. Rama and Adhira believed it was to remember the baby she lost and for the great irresponsibility their father displayed by mortgaging the house that sheltered his pregnant wife and minor children.

Twenty-eight years ago, a different neighbourhood heard Kala scream. None had warned her of the labour pains of the first childbirth.

"Never again, Devi, my dear Goddess, my mother! Save me from this pain!"

Kala cried over and over again. After an agonising 16 hours of torture, a baby girl arrived into this world.

Kala had bled into unconsciousness and would wake up two days later.

The First-Born

Shiva named his firstborn Kamakshi.

Kamakshi and her next two siblings grew up as children of a poor man for the initial years. A wilful child, she was not easy to handle. She never listened to her mother, and her father ensured Kala would not hit her to discipline her. Kamakshi was raised predominantly by her paternal grandmother. Kala was a young mother at 17 years and had much to learn about raising children. It would be years before Kala grew to become the mature matriarch she was.

The mother and child found the distance between each other grow, as the next children came in every few years. The repeated pregnancies and labour and convalescence periods ensured Kala missed out on a significant portion of Kamakshi's growing-up years. Kamakshi was taught to be disrespectful to her mother by her grandmother. This would continue till her last breath.

When Kamakshi was a teen, her father found fortune in the movie industry and she suddenly found herself in possession of the latest styles in her wardrobe. This continued for a while until she was close to marriageable age when the tables turned and her father lost the fortune he made through ill-thought-out decisions.

The riches-to-rags twist of fate left an indelible dent in Kamakshi's memory. She would struggle to earn when she didn't have money, and struggle even more to keep it when she did have money, all her life.

When she turned 18, Kamakshi was married to a Tamil Brahmin typist. Their horoscopes were a perfect match.

The newly married couple tried their hand in multiple small businesses over the years to make ends meet.

They struck gold when their children were growing up having ventured into the goods transport industry. They would play the middlemen and hire vehicles to transport goods from one destination to another.

Kamakshi loved to flaunt her riches.

It is often the absence of something that births a longing for the same.

Kanjeevaram silk saris replaced the simple cotton ones, and her daughter and son dressed in the same fashion as the children shown in movies. Her daughter Sukanya sported the latest hairstyle every year.

Kamakshi hated being poor. She transferred that hate to those who were poor. As her bank balance grew, so did her hate for her parents and siblings.

Jealousy was her second name.

One day, Adhira visited Kamakshi's house with a pack of sweets. She had passed her school board exams with good marks.

Adhira happily opened the packet of sweets and pranced happily around the house distributing the sweets.

Kamakshi took a piece of the coconut *burfi*.

"She has not made this well this time. She is losing her touch." She criticised her own mother's cooking, as she took a bite of the burfi.

Such was her hatred that she had long stopped calling her Amma, and referred to her as 'She'.

"I wonder," Adhira turned around catching a change in the tone of her eldest sibling, "how you passed the exams. Did you cheat, Adhira?"

Adhira's face flushed red and her breath turn rapid and heavy. Her nostrils flared and her eyes started to brim with tears.

"Why would I cheat? Am I not capable of passing the exam?"

Adhira fumed holding back angry tears.

Kamakshi replied, her voice dripping in sweet sarcasm, "Not that. Of course, you can. I paid for the tuition fees of my neighbour's son since they could not afford it. He did not clear the exam, despite tuition. You did not have tuition, so I simply wondered how it was that he failed while you passed. That is all Adhira. It is good. One less burden for your parents. As it is, you younger lot are a big burden to them."

She walked away with a subtle but unmistakable huff and puff.

That night, Adhira cried herself to sleep in her mother's arms instead of staying up to celebrate her victory.

Mithila would visit Kamakshi and her family frequently. Not because she liked any of them much but because she loved the house. There were countless places to hide and many a time she would be in the house for hours and play and Kamakshi would never know. She hated her eldest sister as she made her feel unwelcome and treated her like a "maid servant's daughter", as Mithila would one day as a mother explain the feeling to her daughter.

Sukanya played a lot with Mithila as they were just a few years apart.. Rama, Raghu, and these two girls were good company.

Sukanya was a bit spoiled, as one would expect.

One day in the middle of play, Sukanya held Mithila's long, thick braid that reached her hips and asked her mother, "Amma, make my hair like this. She has such lovely thick hair and look at mine!"

Kamakshi feigned a laugh as the girls went back to play. It was nearing dusk and it would be time for Mithila to head back to her house. Mithila was bidding farewell to Sukanya when Kamakshi stopped her.

The First-Born

"Mithu, wait. What is the hurry dear? Let me comb your hair. It is such a mess."

Mithila was a naïve girl of 12. Pleased by this sudden act of affection by her cold sister, she got a comb and sat on the floor in front of the chair Kamakshi was seated on.

Mithila felt the comb run through her long locks a few times. She let out a cry when it got tangled in her hair a few times.

Kamakshi got up and returned from the kitchen with a pair of scissors hidden behind her.

"Your mother is a stupid woman. No child needs such long hair. You cannot manage this."

Mithila heard a few snips and by the time she turned around, her long locks lay lifeless on the floor. Unlike the straight pattern with few waves on her head, they now were in obnoxious scattered patterns all over the floor where she sat. Mithila in horror took her hand up to her hair the length of which now lay just below her shoulders.

She cried and sobbed the entire way back home to her Amma.

Kala flew into a rage on seeing Mithila, and hit her hard repeatedly, "Why did you let that witch cut your hair? Why did you?"

"Amma, please I did not. She didn't ask me. I didn't know. She was combing my hair she said!" Mithila managed to convey through her sobs and tears.

That night, Mithila had bruises all over her body from the beating. They healed in a week. But the bruises on her soul and that of Kala's would last their lifetime and the future generations who heard the story.

Many years passed. The wounds lay buried in memories, never forgotten.

Adhira called Mithila. "Mithila, Kamakshi is admitted into a hospital. She is seriously ill they say."

They travelled to Kochi to be with their sister. Not every sibling could visit.

Kamakshi died a painful death with multiple small heart attacks over hours.

The body was laid in the spacious living room in the south-north direction, with the feet towards the north. The toes were tied together with a white thread. The body was draped in a white cloth. Flowers were laid over Kamakshi.

The room was a picture of grief: the grief of her children and siblings. Relatives, servants, and neighbours visited to pay their respects.

Adhira and Mithila cried buckets of tears.

Somebody important seemed to have entered the premises as everyone parted to make way.

The First-Born

Kala walked in elegantly in her nine-yards and white blouse. She walked to the lifeless body of her firstborn.

She looked at her face for an entire five minutes. She then simply turned around and looked straight at Adhira and Mithila and their sorry state.

With one glance, the daughters understood they were to follow their mother.

Kala left the house and walked to the courtyard and stopped under the large mango tree near the gate.

She looked calm and composed. She looked as fresh as she would after her morning temple visit. Not a tinge of emotion or sadness could be detected anywhere on her face.

"You fools!"

The daughters looked at their mother in bewilderment. Had she gone crazy hearing the news of her dead child?

"Stop shedding tears now. I expect more of you. Why do you cry for someone so evil? Have you forgotten the atrocities she committed?"

"Stop it Amma! She is our sister and your child! How can you be so cruel and without human emotions?"

"Without emotions? Me? Have you lost your mind Adhira? Did she ever treat you well? Mithila, I cried ten times more when she chopped your hair. You were a child! Was that not cruelty? What about Sharada? Did not her brain-washing wreak havoc in Sharada's married life? Poor Amu ran off and married that white alcoholic boy. Who would not when raised in a house with constant fighting?

Mithila, she was good to you only during the time she had lost money and needed to borrow from your in-laws. How can you forget all this? You disappoint me, both of you.

She never once called me Amma after she became rich. She berated me with my mother-in-law. She knew of our struggles and my condition when we were thrown out of our first home. Did you know she had more than enough money and space in her own house and never offered to help her pregnant mother and siblings her own daughter's age? Am I being cruel here or are you two acting foolish?"

Kala turned around and walked towards the gate. She glanced at the house and entrance one last time. She would never set foot here again.

She held her shoulders and head higher than she had when she came in. She opened the gates wide and walked away calmer than she had ever looked in her entire life.

THE MESSENGER

It was a morning when the birds, including the crows, chose to sing rather than make cacophony like other days. The sun rose earlier than usual, the golden rays engulfed the room in a divine glow. There was no sound of the traffic. Sunday mornings are beautiful, today was even better.

MS Subbalakshmi's voice resonated through the gramophone, and it was a Suprabhatam befitting every God mankind believed in. Vanya though had decided to miss this glorious morning and continued to sleep in, making soft noises now and then. The *puttu* vessel her mother had put on the burner in the background made a gentle whistling sound and lulled her deeper into her slumber. Sukanya Padmanabhan hummed the Suprabhatam along with the legendary singer's recording.

One month in this new home, away from her husband, and with a nine-month-old daughter, she was pleasantly surprised to find that she felt self-sufficient and happy most days. Having never been a homebody, this was an experience she seldom imagined she would have. She had quit her job a year ago and now found herself in a new role as a full-time single mother.

Well, while Sukanya was not divorced or separated per se, she called herself that, as her husband worked in Saudi and came home on fleeting visits once a year. Today, they would be celebrating their fifth wedding anniversary. She kept a count of the number of days she had spent with him since their wedding. It was a total of 186 days in five years. He had seen his daughter just once. He called once every fortnight, and it was the same. A cold greeting, enquiry about their health, whether they needed more money, and that he would plan on coming home soon. There never was any significant emotional connection. Maybe that's what a rushed arranged marriage felt like, she reasoned for mental peace.

Vanya was hence a breath of fresh air in her life. Something that was her entirely.

She and Vanya had all the time in the world to get to know each other and Sukanya was a patient woman; quite unlike her mother Kamakshi. She loved her mother deeply, but she decided to be a more loving mother to her daughter. Kamakshi belonged to an older generation, who never embraced their children. Sukanya had been witness to the contorted and very complicated relationship between her mother and grandmother. A repeat of this history was her greatest fear.

As she undid the cylindrical aluminium contraption and pushed out the steaming puttu on a plate with a plunger, the doorbell rang. It was 8.10 am.

The Messenger

Too early for a visitor. She opened the door and there stood a strapping young man with a beard framing his majestic face. He beamed ear to ear on seeing her. She stood transfixed at this unexpected visitor and looked at him from head to toe. The tips of his maroon leather shoes were muddy, the rest shined and sparkled, his cream trousers well ironed, and the pastel pink shirt added to his masculinity rather surprisingly. He held a bouquet of white lilies in his left hand.

"Sukku manni, are you going to let me in at all?"

"Oh, yes yes. Please come, come on in!" Sukanya opened the door wide to let this tall gentleman come in. He dropped the bunch of lilies in her arms.

"Happy anniversary Manni!"

Sukanya smiled. She rushed to make coffee for him, while he went to see his niece for the first time.

"Bala, here is your coffee. Be careful it's very hot."

Bala sat by the cradle grinning at his chubby niece.

"Any news from Bhadran? When is he planning to return?"

Sukanya looked at him sternly, "He is your brother. You tell me when is he finally returning for good?" Bala shrugged feeling helpless.

"What brings you here suddenly?" she asked, changing the topic, as she arranged the wonderful lilies in a vase in her drab tiny one-roomed house. "These bring a new life to the house, don't they?" She admired the flowers and glanced at her brother-in-law questioningly.

"I remembered your anniversary. I landed last night. I am here for a job interview. If all goes well, I will move in somewhere close and..." He lifted Vanya out of the cradle and swung her up in the air, "...see my little angel grow up!"

The room brimmed with her chuckles as her uncle lifted her high, she flew in the air, and he caught her in his arms as she came down, laughing even louder. Sukanya felt so blessed to witness this sight of pure love and joy and innocence. She went to the kitchen to get Bala some puttu *kadala* curry. She plated the food and turned when she heard a thud, and Vanya cry out aloud.

She dropped the plate and ran out of the compact kitchen to the room.

Bala was frantically trying to console the screaming infant.

"Manni, we were playing and I accidentally lifted her near the beam. It hit her head and then she fell on the ground before I could catch her. I am so sorry."

Bala was on the verge of tears, running all around the room holding the inconsolable baby. Sukanya struggled to grab the child from his arms and rocked her for a long time in her arms. Vanya's face was redder than she had ever seen. She ran her hand through Vanya's head and body. She felt a bump at the left parietal region of the head. Sukanya ran to the fridge and pulled out the ice tray.

"Bala wrap some ice cubes in the towel now!"

She placed the towel filled with ice cubes on the bump. She kept singing and rocking the infant till she stopped wailing. It felt like a long time before the silence.

Bala looked at her with eyes full of tears. Sukanya put the now asleep Vanya back in the cradle. "I am so sorry manni. I didn't mean to..."

"I know I know. But I will need to find a doctor soon. It's Sunday. Won't be an easy task. I better have her checked."

"I'll come with you..."

"No, no... don't worry. She is asleep now. I will make some calls and figure it out. You may take leave and get settled. All the best for your interview tomorrow, Bala."

Bala left with a heavy heart.

Sukanya went back to check on her daughter. Vanya was sleeping peacefully, with no sign of the trauma. The sun was shining high up in the sky now. The room felt warm and Sukanya drew the curtains. The flat was just below the terrace and she had predicted this problem of it getting extremely hot in summer. But she needed a house at short notice. The last landlord was very unforgiving and the rent was higher than she could now afford, especially with a newborn.

She made herself a cup of coffee to calm her nerves and sat with her phone diary. She sorely missed her mother. Kamakshi was at her best in times of crisis. She would always know what to do when everyone else panicked.

Her slender index finger turned the rotating dial of the phone gracefully. She called the clinics of the few child specialists she knew. The calls went unanswered. Exasperated, she called the last hospital on the list, St Mary's Hospital, asking for a paediatrician. "Sorry madam, no one is available today. Can you come tomorrow?"

"My baby has had a head injury, mam. It's an emergency. Please help!"

"Is she bleeding? Is she conscious?"

"No, there is no blood. She is fine. She is asleep now. She did cry a lot after the fall though. And yes, I can feel a bump on top of her head."

"Mam, in that case, it is best that you bring the child over to our emergency services immediately. The medical officers there will assess her."

Sukanya finished the coffee in one gulp and packed her handbag. She pulled out a soft wrap for Vanya and wrapped it around her. Vanya's hand fell out of the wrap. Sukanya held her tiny fingers to push it back again. She shuddered when the child's fingers felt cold.

She ran her hands on her forearm, it felt cold as well. She parted the child's clothes and felt her stomach. The stomach was warmer but there was no up-down motion of the stomach or chest with every breath. Sukanya felt the blood drain from her face. She touched the bump on Vanya's head. It felt larger than before. Significantly. She picked up the child and shook her, but Vanya wouldn't wake up. Her toes were cold as well. She ran with the child to the window. She pulled apart the eyelids and noticed the eye on the side of the bump had a dilated pupil. Cold sweat broke out on her forehead. She kept her ear on the child's chest. The silence within was deafening.

This can't be happening. No! No! No!

She slumped to the ground and placed Vanya on her lap. Internally, she was screaming in horror, but not a sound passed her lips.

Her heartbeat rose higher and higher, her palms began sweating. Sukanya started to lose her vision, everything turned black and she slumped to the floor with a soft thud losing consciousness.

The birds sang their song with unusual joy this morning. The sun's golden rays filled the room with a divine glow.

Sukanya opened her eyes to find herself on her bed. An early riser, she must have missed the alarm today. MS Subbalakshmi's voice resonated in the room. How? She had not turned on the gramophone.

Sukanya was confused as she got out of bed. As her feet hit the ground, her memory jolted her back to reality, she gasped and sprang out to rush to the cradle at the foot end of the bed. Vanya was as still as she was before the blackout. She picked up the child in haste. To her shock, the child cried loudly and complained about being woken up so rudely. She placed the infant on the bed and undid her clothes. Vanya's eyes were open, she kicked in irritation, her eyes were teary, her body felt warm, and her fingers curled around her mother's and pushed it away. All Vanya wished for is to sleep soundly without such impolite disturbances.

Confounded and disoriented, Sukanya walked around looking at the room. She then remembered, rushed back to the bed and ran her hand on Vanya's head. There was no bump either.

She sat on the floor holding her head wondering if she was still sane.

The doorbell rang.

The Messenger

She looked at the clock. It was 8.10 a.m. She opened the door to find a strapping young man with a beard framing his majestic face. He wore a pastel pink shirt and beige coloured well-ironed trousers.

"Happy anniversary Manni!" he said as he entered the house and gave her the beautiful pink lotus flower that he held in his right hand.

MEMORY LANES

I was two when we played hide and seek.

He always knew where I hid,

But never did let on and allowed his effort to seem meek.

I turned ten and we would go on evening walks.

Not a man of many words,

We would enjoy *kulfi* and fill in the silences in our talks.

I blossomed at 18 and it was time to leave home.

He hated that but did not say a word.

We both recognised the sacrifice it would take and we were prepared to carry the pain.

It was in my 25th year that I brought a boy home for him to meet.

He stayed silent through the meal.

I was not worried, as I knew it would take more than just one meeting.

I was 30 when he got that fateful call.

Rushed to the hospital did he to see my mangled mass.

Sitting beside me, night and day, little did he know that I knew it all.

On my 40th, I got him, my much-awaited newborn, to see.

His eyes widened beneath the thick heavy brows,

Lift his grandson did he, as proud as a king would be,

Today, on my 50th birthday, I sit beside him, holding his wrinkled hand.

This man next to me is a mere shadow of his former majestic self.

The smile long lost, he asks, "Adhira, where is Amma? I am hungry."

I fetch him food from the kitchen; he does not complain, calling it bland.

Adhira was his elder sister and his Amma has been gone for years,

I hide away and pull back my tears with all my might.

TEN PAISA

Changanassery Vaidyanathan was an immensely popular Ayurvedic doctor in Ernakulam.

He was originally from Changanassery town in the Kottayam district but had moved to Ernakulam as a child with his gifted father who was a herbal healer himself. The name of the town stuck and he was called thus all his life.

Vaidyanathan counted words as he spoke. The maximum he may have spoken to a patient might have been 12 words.

The patient sat on a stool near his table in his tiny clinic. The patient voiced his or her issues: stomach ache, fever, vomiting, and others. Vaidyanathan would then put forward his hand. The patients would stretch out their hands to let him check their pulse. For most patients, this is all that was needed to make a diagnosis and write the prescription. At times he would ask them to open their mouth and put out their tongue and say "Aaaah". He could diagnose causes of fever, anaemia, pregnancy, causes of headaches, high blood pressure, and deficiencies simply by feeling the pulse. The throat and tongue were simply confirmatory tools. The stethoscope lay on the table gathering dust.

The sceptics would also be at rest once they experienced how truly effective his medicines and diagnosis would be. Armed with a proper medical college degree, Vaidyanathan's fame exceeded that of his self-taught healer father. He would personally monitor the preparation of the medicines sold at his clinic. His knowledge of Ayurvedic herbs surpassed what he was taught in medical school with additions from his lineage of healers.

Kala was not easily impressed. Vaidyanathan diagnosed and treated her unrelenting headache some years ago. Ever since he was the only doctor Kala ever went to. Over time, Vaidyanathan had become very familiar with Kala's constitution and her frequent headaches and stomach aches. Vaidyanathan's clinic was around eight km away from where Kala lived.

As time passed, she stopped visiting the good doctor when she was in severe pain, but would instead send one of her children. "Go to Vaidyanathan and tell him Amma has a stomach ache and bring me medicines."

Kala would hand over money and a small bag to the child for the long walk.

This particular season was Mithila's turn to go to the doctor to collect medicine for Kala. The elder siblings were in Mumbai with their father, the younger ones were busy in higher classes in school, and Raghu was too young with a tendency to be disobedient.

Mithila was a tender seven years old and forced to carry out this 'doctor duty' for quite a few years.

Mithila disliked walking such a long distance in the hot sun. The only beautiful sight for her was passing by the candy store. The stairs up to the doctor's room were high. She had to climb over each one in the colonial-style government hospital building, using her hands and feet. She used to dread doctors and hospitals. It is ironic that decades later her child would become one. Kala would give Mithila 10 paisa to buy candy on the way back. That was her only motivation for the long taxing walk.

Mithila awaited her turn in the hour-long queue. She entered the doctor's tiny consulting room.

"Kala's girl, right? Headache, backache or stomachache?"

"Stomachache Vaidyanathan sir."

He wrote a prescription and asked the child to hand it over to his assistant outside at the medicine dispensing counter. Mithila picked up the medicine.

"Careful my child, do not let the bottle fall.", said the compounder.

The government hospital provided free consultations and medicines to all.

She headed back home. Her pace was always faster on the journey back. As she reached closer to

Ten Paisa

the candy shop, she stepped down from the footpath to cross the street. In one hand, she carried the small bag with the bottle of medicine and dug deep in her pocket with the other for the 10 paisa coin. Mithila pulled out the coin and gleamed at it, walking towards the tiny candy store. She was a few feet away from the shop. She could see the jar of orange candy that was shaped like miniature slices of orange, the strawberry-shaped sugar candy that had a plastic leaf sticking out and would be white inside with a smearing of the red external colour creating shades of pink with each bite, the coin-shaped peppermint candy, oval mango candy, the cigarette shaped candy in red packets with a picture of the Phantom on the cover. She tried to make up her mind about what she would purchase. She ensured she ate and finished the candy before she reached home, lest her brothers grab them.

A burly man bumped harshly into this little engrossed child. Time slowed down for her, as she saw the coin fall out of her hand, roll along the footpath, towards the corner and through the iron bars covering a tiny drain.

Mithila did not bother to look for the man who bumped into her but ran following her coin. Alas, there was nothing she could do to stop its journey into the gutter.

Mithila sat by the side of the gutter with tears streaming down her face. All this effort for nothing.

She cried so much that everything appeared blurry. She felt a hand on her right shoulder and looked up. Through the teary haze, she could see a man in a light blue shirt. The same colour as the shop owner was wearing. She quickly wiped her eyes to get a better look and got up.

It was the shop owner indeed.

He handed her a packet that required both her hands. She placed the medicine bottle on the ground and accepted the packet. She opened the paper a little to find an array of all the candies that were in the shop!

Oh, what delight! She smiled wide and looked at the kind man with her tear-stained face. The smile immediately was wiped away as she realised, she didn't have money for this.

"*Molé* (daughter), take this with you and don't cry. This is for you, no need to pay. Go home now. It is getting late. And walk carefully and be extra careful with money next time, my child."

He hastened back to manage the customers in his shop.

Mithila stood there staring at the candy in her hand for a few moments. She grabbed the bag with the medicine bottle and held on to the precious candy tightly with both hands, and walked back home the happiest girl in the world.

LUCK, DESTINY OR FATE?

"Jonathan!!"

She gasped, nearly dropping the bag she was holding, and with her other hand, she covered her open mouth.

He stopped in his tracks frozen and took a few moments before he turned around to face her.

That face was just as lovely, even more so, except that the hair was shorter. She also had some laugh lines at the corner of her eyes. He smiled to himself, realising that she must have had a good life.

"*Kanna* (dear)...", he whispered and held out an open palm to hold her hand.

"Jonathan *anna...anna...inge...epudi? Avalo varsham...*(Brother...here...how? So many years...)"

She struggled to catch her breath. As he cradled her cold hand, she appeared to calm down and gather her emotions.

"Would you have time for a cup of coffee, Amu?"

Soon, two lost souls were seen walking from the supermarket with bags in their hands to the coffee shop on the opposite side of the street.

Stories My Grandma Never Told Me

"How long have you been here, Kanna?"

"It's been two years now. I was in America before that. I spent 14 years there and then moved here with my husband. You see he is German, and he always wanted to return home… What about you Anna? Tell me everything! Murthy, Amma, we all thought you died in that…"

Her voice was drowned out by the mere memory of that pain.

She drew a deep breath.

"*Enna aacha* (what happened)? Murthy searched high and low for you. *Teriyamaa* (did you know)?"

Her accusatory tone didn't go unmissed.

"Where do I begin? Hmmm… I was already a member of the association when I came to live with your family in the 1980s. I think Murthy suspected but I respect him for never asking. I found great peace and love in your family in Kumbakonam. Who would have thought an Iyer family in Kumbakonam would shelter a Sri Lankan Tamil Christian revolutionary?"

He laughed.

"Well, you did not know. Yet…I deeply appreciate that. It was a very turbulent time and too risky for me to stay in my country."

He had a few sips of water.

Luck, Destiny Or Fate?

"When I returned home, things were looking up. Our leader was hopeful, the plans foolproof. But unbeknownst to us, there were internal factions in the ideology. Our association started to recruit children, and some of us who protested were asked to stay silent. The attacks increased and so did the 'do or die' philosophy. The army in retaliation started brutally attacking our villages and killing people randomly: man, woman, and child.

Our beautiful land was a mess – debris, dust and dead bodies.

Then one fine day, they killed your then-prime minister. Then began the worst nightmare!

My brother Selvaraj was amongst the ones killed in a forest hideout round-up. Selva was a very promising upcoming leader. A brilliant strategist in guerrilla methodology. His death was an important turning point in the war, especially for our subdivision. Needless to say, I was a broken man. Selva was everything to me, a father figure to an orphan like me."

His voice choked.

"I was married a few years before that to a fellow revolutionary named Mariyam. Both of us were at the hospital when we heard the news that our village had been vandalised by the army and everyone was killed. At that time we found out she was pregnant. Are you a parent kanna?"

"Yes, Anna. I have a nine-year-old son," she beamed.

The counter announced, "Coffee for Matthew!"

Jonathan got up and picked up the coffee.

"Changed your name or was that just for coffee?"

Jonathan grinned.

"One thing at a time."

They had a few sips of coffee in silence.

"This attack on my village occurred barely six months after Selva died. I was still grieving and my comrades were dying in droves. When we came to know about the pregnancy, everything changed. We went into hiding, staying in a trusted friend's house for some weeks, keeping away from every door and window.

A month later, I went to see the ruins of my village. In the dead of the night. Amritha, Amu, *kanna, enna solla?* (what is there to tell?)

Everything was destroyed. Everything! Thata and my sister, our innocent neighbours, their children. All gone. There were bullet holes on the walls that were still standing…

Some metres away was a large pit with fresh mud: a mass grave, for souls that were living and breathing some days ago, who laughed, loved and cried. Most of them had nothing to do with us and our association."

Amritha held his trembling hands.

"I got scared, kanna. I was defeated in body, mind and soul."

Amritha's eyes brimmed with tears. She had never known Jonathan to cry or even be disheartened.

"I gathered a handful of earth from my courtyard and from over the grave and left. In the next few weeks, I sold whatever jewellery my wife was wearing to get a pass in a boat and we headed to Indonesia. There have since been immense struggles and moving from country to country, trying to erase every trace of our past. All for that unborn child. We were parents now."

He beamed.

"We had a long journey over the years, from Indonesia, Malaysia, and Thailand. We then moved to Ukraine. From there, Germany. Germany has been home for seven years. I could say that I might spend the rest of my life here."

"What work are you doing now?"

"Oh yes, I remember you used to call me a painter as a child. I am good at numbers too you see. I met a fine Tamil gentleman while in Thailand. He had multiple businesses and needed a good trusted accountant and manager. I started working for him and became his right-hand man which took us to Ukraine and now this country. I can't complain. Time has been kind to me....

Enough about me, *nee epudi irukkai* (how are you?) How are Murthy, uncle and aunty? How is *paati* (grandmother)?"

"They are all fine anna. Murthy remembers you often, especially on your birthday and during Pongal. Amma has some joint pain issues and does not venture out much these days. Appa is healthy and active. Paati is even better. She is 89 years and still draws kolam at the entrance of the house every day!"

"Paati refused to let me paint her when she had come over during your board exams. She asked me why did I wish to paint someone so old!"

Amritha laughed imagining her grandmother Kala's expression at that odd request.

"Anna, do you remember how much Amma used to scold and hit me for all the mistakes I made in maths? You would reason with her and take her away and calm her down. You recognised my dyslexia when no one else could. As also my flair for art which lay buried deep within."

Amritha showed him some paintings and sculpture pictures on her phone.

"Are these your works?"

"Yes, anna. I kept painting and honing my skills even after you left. In fact, I still have all the books and drawings you did to teach me. I studied in Mumbai and later did my masters in Fine Arts in the U.S. and that's where I met my husband Frank.

You gave me this life. You showed me what could be. I would have been stuck in that village as a wife or a frustrated failed engineer in Chennai or Bangalore had you not come into our lives!"

Jonathan picked up their empty coffee mugs and put them away.

"Amu, that little girl... What was her name? The one who learned calligraphy from me? Was a little brat that one, but very sharp. Did she become a doctor? She would keep talking of becoming a surgeon all day remember?"

"Chitra! Oh yes, she has recently finished her internship. She did become a doctor. Still a brat she is!" Amu laughed talking of her cousin.

As they walked to the door, he spoke in a mellow tone.

"I changed my name to Matthew when I landed in Indonesia. The government books in Sri Lanka count me as one of the dead.

It has been hard, kanna. I still feel guilty that I left my motherland. But now my focus is the safety of my son. We are lucky to stay alive! I do not know if this is luck, fate or destiny still. Maybe I am just meant to protect my son and it's not in my fate to give my life for my land. I will never find out.

As a parent, I am sure you understand. As for art, I am glad you took it up. I don't paint anymore. I stopped after Selva's death. But do you know I painted an abstract with the earth I picked up from my home? It stays framed in my living room."

"Murthy especially will be so happy to know that you are alive and well."

"Regarding that... I would rather he not know. Meeting you brings the past alive. And my pain is intense. If you do tell Murthy, ask him not to contact me though. I cannot bear it anymore."

Amritha understood.

As they parted ways, they knew full well that they may never see each other ever again. She asked, "What is your child's name, anna?"

"Selvaraj."

Jonathan...Matthew pulled up the collar of his jacket high and walked away into the snowy evening blizzard mingling with the crowd.

Amritha stood transfixed staring in his direction until her phone started to ring.

"Hello, yes Frank. Yes, yes. I shall head there right away."

She sat in her car and drove quickly to pick up her son Jonathan from his ballet lessons.

ONE LIFE, TWO LOVES

The blinding sunlight reflected on the pristine white snow. The crisp chilly wind was blowing against my face. I could no longer feel my frozen nose. I felt a smile emerge on my face.

Kargil seemed like a cosy little valley from atop the high mountainous roads. Dotted with coloured houses amongst winding lanes and interspersed with trees against a backdrop of snow-capped mountains, Kargil was as pretty as a postcard. A strapping young man in his early twenties drove us from Srinagar to Kargil.

Ali.

He appeared light-footed and was not very tall. There was a casual nonchalant manner about the way he walked and talked. He appeared to not have a care in this world, the kind that would make one shouldering multiple responsibilities of this world, envious. He squinted his eyes against the sunlight as he spoke, his hair looked like he had just gotten up from bed. I could not imagine him with combed hair though. The checked shirt with collar button undone and the rolled up sleeves, the well-worn out jeans, seemed to have accompanied him in his many travels. His sports shoes were covered in layers of dust and mud. But his smile that welcomed you ran from ear to ear and you knew at once you were in the presence of a man who knew what it was to be truly happy. He apologized for being late. He was held up by his wife and young son who had accompanied him to Srinagar to visit a relative before receiving us at the airport.

His driving was rash. Yet the confidence he displayed and the control he had of his car was such, I never felt like asking him to slow down. He was quiet at first. After a stop for brunch, it was my turn to sit next to the driver. In two minutes of sitting there, out spilt Ali's story. He was the second son of a simple couple in a village five km from Kargil. Due to financial issues, he and his brother had to quit school and take up driving to fend for their family. He already had eight years of experience driving. Gradually he told me more interesting parts of his story. He was in love with a girl in the neighbourhood since childhood.

They assumed they would get married one day when they would grow up. But alas, his parents had other plans. When he turned 18, they asked him to marry a girl they chose from another village. In the traditional mindset, pressure and fear of going against his parent's wishes, he had to succumb and marry this girl. He remembered vividly how much his love had cried on hearing this. Not once did she ask him why he didn't go against their wishes. Not once did she label him a cheat, a heartbreaker. All she did was silently wipe away the tears flowing from her two lovely eyes. The pain was so very palpable in the air. He couldn't look at her pained broken eyes any longer and quietly walked out in the eerie silence.

He was married three weeks later.

He saw her face for the first time on the wedding night. In the next few weeks, he came to know his bride as a shy, understanding woman who rarely questioned him about his whereabouts. The only fault he noticed was that she would get up late and was slow at housework. He ignored that at first but then in a month post marriage he started nagging her about how slow she was. But the scolding seemed to fall on deaf ears, it seemed, she had not changed a bit in the last five years!

After two years or so, he was driving some tourists and stopped at a little obscure village that he had been passing by for all these years, but never bothered to stop at. A little girl was sick and vomiting and he had to stop at the village for water and medicines. He was strolling around while the anxious parents tried to comfort their little girl. The village appeared to be located on a higher level than his. The lanes were winding with many up hills and down hills. He walked towards the marketplace. He passed kids playing hopscotch on the winding streets. Boys were playing cricket at a tiny clearing in the vicinity of the busy marketplace.

He stopped at the apricot section where the sellers were calling out to customers to come and buy at their stall. He suddenly had an odd feeling, a feeling of familiarity. He turned around to look back at the street as if some unknown force made him do that. He saw a woman in her 20s go by on the other side of the street. She was wearing a Pashmina shawl over a traditional deep maroon dress that her tribe wore that covered her to her ankles. Her expression was grim. She seemed like one would not smile easily. Her cheeks were pink against the black of the shawl. Her tiny eyes hid what she was thinking. A gush of emotions passed through Ali's mind. He could not take his eyes away from her. Memories, happy memories that now seemed as painful as a thousand knives piercing through his chest, engulfed him. Before he realised it, he was following her at the same slow pace a few metres away. Each step was getting heavier with the weight of the emotions he felt, with his mind travelling back and forth in the past. He remembered the times when he would stop by her window acting like he was repairing his car, just to glance at her standing by her window with her hair left open, each time checking to see if her brothers were at the door. How time and events in life can turn the most joyous of memories into pure pain and tragedy.

Her gait was still the same. The subtle limp on the left that only people who knew her very well could identify. It was the same gait as her fathers'. Their left leg was a few inches shorter than the right.

She took a sharp turn to the left on exiting the marketplace. The lane went uphill. Numbed by the multitude of emotions he felt, he had to remember to breathe. It felt like ages ago when he held her hand for the first time and found that they were very rough due to the daily washing, and cleaning she helped her mother with. Despite that, for him, those were the most beautiful hands in the world. In the right universe, he still would be holding them on his own. He kept walking behind her as if in a spell.

He thought back to the time he sat waiting for her behind the tiny cottage in the apple orchard hiding from the village. It was March and the orchard was in full bloom. He was impatient. After what seemed an eternity, she came in like a dream, floating across the flowering trees, dancing her way through, adding more beauty to the already scenic view. Her pink cheeks would put to shade the loveliness of the soon-to-fruit apples in the orchard. She sat next to him and opened the picnic basket she carried. He tasted the dessert she had made of milk and a meat dish mildly spiced with pepper. While the food was lovely, her beauty distracted him.

Today as he followed her across the never-ending twists and turns, he could taste every spoonful of the dessert he had once upon a time.

Well past the main village, they were now on the outskirts. She opened a small green gate that could only fit two people at a time and entered a small garden. He stopped a few metres away and saw her enter a tiny dark cottage. The front door closed and he saw a light flicker inside and a hand placed a candle stick at the table, which could be viewed from the window. Her face appeared like that of an angel by the candlelight. As she disappeared from view, he sat there on a rock looking at the little brown cottage for a long time. As it got darker, he saw her back at the window. She blew out the candle. The moonlight shone upon the dark village now. Countless stars studded the clear skies. The wind carried stories of faraway regions and whistled in his ears. He could not feel the cold against his bones. He was still at a time that was long gone.

On a similar silent night, long ago, he had thrown stones at her window to wake her up. She had come and opened the door. He took her for a short drive. During the entire drive, her expression kept changing from excitement to fear. Her face betrayed the excitement at being with her lover and doing something prohibited, fear of being caught and punished severely. He stopped beyond the outskirts of the village and they sat close together on a small rock like the one he was sitting on now. The cold air failed to extinguish the warmth of the two hands of two individuals in love. She glanced up to see the trillion stars and had a smile on her face that defined bliss and joy. A joy that seemed to transcend space and time. He was not looking at the stars. He could see them in her lovely eyes that were wider

One Life, Two Loves

than he had ever seen them. The very short drive was soon over and she walked quietly back to her home. Fortunately, her absence went unnoticed.

The face he saw today was beautiful but devoid of that excitement and bliss he was once used to. He sat on that rock looking at her home for a long, long time. He wanted to cry at what happened, he wished to comprehend what happened, he tried to think but drew a blank. He gave in and did not stop the tears from flowing. Tears that had gathered over two years. What he tried to forget and put aside, every emotion sprung up and he cried. He cried over what he lost, over what he could not have.

It was soon daybreak and he dragged his heavy feet but lighter heart back to where his car was. He could not find the family who had driven with him. Once home, his mother informed him that his boss had called and thrown him out of his job. The tourists had tried calling him and had to take another car and leave. Nothing bothered him now. He felt like a man who lost and refound the greatest treasure.

He went to his room to find his wife cleaning the cabinet. He ignored her and went to take a shower. He was very quiet for the next few days. One day, while he was driving, he intentionally took the route to the home of his old love. He stopped his car at the door. A twinge of pain hit his heart as he looked at the same window where he often had seen the beautiful girl smiling at him. Now there was no one at the window, and the paint on the window sill was peeling off. Maybe the window too was grieving her absence. He restarted his car and drove on, unable to find the courage to face that home and family. But, after a few metres, he suddenly turned his car around and firmly planted his car right in front of the door of the blue house and turned off the ignition, got out and stood in front of the door and knocked. The moment he knocked; he regretted it. He turned around, but there already was someone unlocking the door. He turned back to see a shrivelled old woman. Her eyes were crinkled at the edges which made her look like she was smiling even when she was not. He introduced himself by his father's name who was well-known in the area as a social and helpful man. She was her grandmother. He entered their home for the first time. There was only her grandmother and mother at home. She made tea for him and offered him homemade biscuits. He told her he was a school friend of their daughter and asked about her whereabouts. Her mother looked sad at the mere mention of her name. She told him she had gone to the nearby village where she worked as a part-time teacher in a primary school. "So, she married and moved away?"

"Well... Not yet. But she will be married very soon," said her mother.

Ali could sense her voice wavering a little on the topic of her daughter.

He nevertheless did not prod further. He thanked them and left for his home. He did not fail to glance at the window and looked at the floor where she used to stand. How gifted was the piece of earth to have kissed her feet so many times...!

He drove aimlessly around the countryside. On returning he met some of their common school friends and started to ask about her. He had not been in touch with his friends since his marriage and driving had kept him very busy the last two years. They were playing a game of cards over tea and he casually asked about old friends who have moved away. He mentioned seeing his old love's mother in the marketplace and wondered how she was doing. His friends looked at each other and stayed silent. He asked, "What is the matter? Tell me now!"

One of his friends, very reluctantly said, "Well Ali, we thought you would eventually come to know. If you did not, it was even better. After your marriage, she was depressed and her family was very worried. But they did not know why she was depressed. They had started looking for suitable grooms. She refused them all and did not meet a single one. When someone would come home, she would misbehave and tell them to get out of the house. Soon she stopped getting suitors. She could not take the nagging at home any longer. So, one day, she told her parents she had got a job in the next village and left. They have been calling her but it seems she does not wish to marry nor does she wish to be in touch with her family. She doesn't even take money from her father or brothers. I am sorry Ali; we just thought it was not a good idea to tell you this since you were married and were still getting over her."

Ali looked lost and grew more emotional on hearing the turn of events. He got up and started towards his car. His friend screamed out, "Ali! You are a married man. Forget all that I told you and carry on with your life as a respectable man."

Ali was depressed for many days. His wife noticed the change and grew worried. The Ali she knew was noisy, and fun and would get into silly arguments with her often. One day, she took him into confidence and asked him, "What is the matter? What is bothering you? I can no longer stand your silence and be a mute witness."

Ali couldn't find the strength to confess. But Isa was a persistent woman and, he relented. At the risk of causing a permanent strain in their relationship, he told her what happened, about his past, how he saw his former lover again, what he had heard about what had become of her.

Isa was silent for a long time. At no time did her face betray any sentiment or emotion she felt. She did not come to bed that night. Ali did not sleep either. The night was a long lonely one.

One Life, Two Loves

The next day, Ali woke up and got ready. Isa served breakfast and they ate in silence. Ali didn't meet her eyes. He felt guilty; he felt he had betrayed not one but two women.

He felt only death could relieve and lift him from the throes of depression and misery.

He walked towards his car. His boss had called him again about his job. Ali was a good driver, despite being rash, there was never a dent or scratch on his car. He shut the car door, turned on the ignition and was about to start when he heard Isa call him. . She bent down to reach his car window and handed him a cream-coloured Pashmina shawl, delicately embroidered with intricate flower patterns at the edges. She whispered looking into his eyes, "Give this to her."

It took a moment for Ali to realize whom she meant. He was shocked. She calmly looked straight into his eyes and said, "I know what I am asking you to do. I know what a broken heart feels like."

Ali had never felt so much respect for his wife nor had he felt such remorse. He did not ask her for any further explanation. Her determined look revealed the introspection that went into such a dramatic decision.

By this time, we had reached a tiny obscure village. The paths were narrower than those of the previous one where we started our ride. The marketplace was a din. Ali dropped us off at a little place that he said had the best tea in the district. There was an apricot stall opposite and we could hear children playing in the nearby ground. It seemed like they were playing cricket. I joined the children for a few minutes. It had been ages since I talked, played and laughed so much. Ladakh had this spiritual quality that served just right at this juncture of my life. I came here to be healed from the hurt of my divorce and the abuse. My last trip to my country before I moved back to America. But Ali reminded me of someone who was in my life years before my husband.

Once we were seated, Ali was walking back to the car and I followed. I caught up with him and asked where he was going and to join us for tea instead. He smiled and told me to come along with him. He climbed a small wall next to the shop and told me to do the same. He pointed uphill in the northeast direction. I could see a tiny brown cottage with a faded green gate that seemed to enclose a tiny garden. "Madam, there is a cup of tea made by the most beautiful hands in the world waiting for me. I shall see you in an hour..."

Like a man who had come in possession of the most desired treasure on earth, he walked to his car with a spring in each step, leaving me on the wall staring at that beautiful humble cottage where someone was brewing aromatic tea. I caught a whiff of that tea, of love in the crisp cold air that day.

THE FINAL LETTER

Dear Jonathan and Margaret,

It's finally time.

I hope I am actually dead and not on life support or in a coma, now that you have broken into the vault.

Last year, as Dr Bryan pronounced my death sentence, I had plenty of time to think. During the third chemo I took, I decided to pen this letter for you two.

Jon, if you have found this ensure Margaret reads it too. The same goes for you, Margie! This is not the time for your bitter superfluous tiffs!

I'll haunt you if you won't!

Where was I? Yes, I wanted to share some truths, some wisdom, and some facts. I agree with what everyone said, I was never the typical mum to either of you.

It was hard to be. I was raised in a village in southern India, was one of the first women in my family to study abroad, pick up a subject that was not maths or biology, and the first to marry a white man too!

Parenting is hard. It gets even more challenging when raising children with two diametrically opposite parenting styles like Frank and I had.

You have met paati, and you have met gammy. The difference was obvious!

Do I have regrets? Well, until a certain age yes, I did. But once I crossed that threshold and stopped trying to please everyone, including myself I was at peace.

That would be pretty much the time I divorced your father and you both started to blame me for every mess in your lives. To date and maybe beyond! Frank did adore you both. But he never did provide for any of us. The unending bottles of whiskey, that came in a few years after you were born Margie, didn't help. That's where Theodore came into the picture. I married Theodore after leaving your father when I realised how difficult it was to raise two children alone. Theo provided for your meals, and your education and was my security for my old age.

I could not return to India with two mixed-race kids. India back then was a different place than what it is today, understand that. And I felt I had no career opportunities there with my art. It would have given a chance for Murthy uncle and Amma to comment and chide me on my choice of a partner. They had cut off all communication for the first three years after I married Frank. Jonathan, your birth was the reason my family reconnected with me, did I ever tell you this?

The Final Letter

You hated that we moved to the States from Germany as well. But now in hindsight, I am certain you realise it was a better choice for us all. Both of you did not forget your German thankfully.

I understand your persistent hate for Theo. But I didn't mind his womanising ways. So long as he didn't bring any of his women home, paid the bills, financed your education, and ensured I had money to refill the jars and the fridge, I didn't care.

There was no love between us and you sensed that better than we could hide it. That blame lay on us as husband-wife.

That doesn't matter now. You grew up well I'd say. Despite the mess that your parents were.

I was a bitter teen and a rebel in my 20s, I guess I have the privilege of blaming that on the terrible relationship my parents had.

I remember the day as yesterday when I discovered I was pregnant with you, Jon. I was terrified and cried for three days. Maybe you sensed it, as by day four something in me changed. I felt calmer and stronger than ever. I threw out my cigarette stash the same night. And I didn't touch alcohol until I had both of you and Margie was in her late teens.

I was overwhelmed when I had you, Jon. I forgot all about the pain the moment I laid my eyes on your little pixie face. Oh, how blessed I felt and how very beautiful the world seemed to have you in my arms and Frank next to me!

I often told you, "Life is what happens when you are busy planning for it."

Margaret was a surprise to me and Frank. Unlike Jon, Margie, you did not let us sleep a wink for months together!

Those initial 10 or 12 years were so wonderful, right? Tiny neat cottage with that white picket fence, mum in an apron and kids running in the small green yard and dad returning home at sunset after work, all of us sitting together for the evening meals.

If I could I would freeze myself in one of those evenings for eternity!

Who could fathom how things would change for us all during one of those sunsets? Life has other plans and unfortunately, over time, we all have taken different paths.

Did either of you feel lonely along the way? I did many times. I now wish I had called you more often and maybe confided in how I felt.

I remain that vain proud lady willing to 'stay strong' even when my legs give way. The lessons life gave, sadly never did enough to teach me to be kinder to myself.

Frank leaving us caught you by surprise. That blame lies on me. I did my best to hide what a terrible husband

and father he was to us all in the later years with his incessant drinking. I made up for his absences and hid his affairs with other women. But it got to a point where I could no longer bear the alcoholism and depression, and I apologise, for the fact that you had to see the nasty divorce when you were in your early teens.

I think that period was the start of the rift between us all as a family.

Think what you may, Theo saved us all. Always be grateful to him for that. I can die in peace knowing you may not forgive me. But him, let go.

When you both left home for university, I could sense my downfall beginning. Theo and I never had that special connection I had with Frank in our early days together.

You two made me so proud of whatever and everything you did in school. I am a proud mama. Except for a few matters.

I do wish that Jon could have joined Yale instead of Northwestern. Your career would have been smoother, my boy. Never mind.

Margie, I do love Emmett so very much. At times I find it hard to believe half his genes come from that silly-looking chap you call your husband.

I am not going to hold either against you and have ensured most of Theo and my wealth is distributed between both of you.

I lived a good life I would say. While I never found lasting love in both my husbands, who found greater love in bottles of whiskey and the beds of other women; I don't want you to pity me. During your tempestuous 20s and teens before that, I admit to eavesdropping multiple times outside your doors. I was essentially a single mother and had to look after two children. Theo was always travelling for his many businesses.

Jon, in the later years, I saw through your struggles with Julia, and how you left her after you caught her cheating on you. I remember the night you came home instead of going to your apartment and cried in my lap. I felt blessed to be a mother and wished I could take away all your pain.

Margie, you are a beautiful, kind, intelligent woman. Don't let anyone tell you otherwise. You tend to act rash and stupid at times. Rob is an example of your stupidity. But for sweet little chubby Emmett!

What I am to reveal next may come as a shock to you.

But well, I always did tell you this,

'There are liars in this world. They say men lie more. But remember one is a liar only if caught.'

Theo didn't matter much. I was loved by a few men and I made my peace with the arrangement. Theo just never found out. I wish to repay their families a tad, for I have a great fondness for these men. I have mentioned their names in the will.

The Final Letter

Just so you don't ask questions during the reading, I am mentioning some details here.

Jake used to visit us 15 years ago for plumbing issues. Jake is no more. But I have given a small amount to his daughter.

Old William next door has been a darling all these years. Give him the said amount in cash. His wife is very smart. We had a hard time keeping everything a secret from Grace.

Jackson Blackmore runs a tiny bookstore at the 63rd and 46th cross junction. No one buys books these days. An extremely intelligent passionate man of words, I owe him some of my most beautiful memories. Much of the books you read as children were his gifts. Be kind to him and buy Emmett books instead of iPads and laptops please, Margie!

Jon and Margie, always be there for each other. You two have been my greatest treasures.

We have fought, not spoken for days at times, but I always loved you.

Don't judge me like you did Theo. Everyone has reasons. I had mine.

In all, I lived a good life. I die a happy woman.

Margie, please join the workforce again once Emmett is a little older. He will grow up the proud child of a working mother and you will find that Rob respects you more when you bring in money. Needless to say, you will have your independence in life to do as you please and take decisions.

Jon, marry by all means if you wish to, if not it's still fine. But remember to judge people less. Never forget, we all lie.

It's just that women are better liars and far more accomplished at taking secrets to the grave!

Good luck and live full lives my darlings and don't mind the random blabbering of a dying woman on chemo. Oh well, now dead hopefully. You better not keep me on life support!

Always and forever,

Your loving ma,

Amritha.

THE FIRST CUT

Thud!

Her head slowly slumped as she slid to the floor. She felt a gush of warm liquid on her face. The scene appeared blurred as the fluid filled her eyes and oozed down her head and face. She could barely make out the human form in front of her and the vague outlines of the dining table. A human voice shouted words, but they seemed faint compared to her harsh gasping breaths and pounding chest. It took her several moments to realize her face was being bathed in her blood from the injury on her head that left a gaping wound on her scalp. She could not feel pain. She could not think. Maybe this was what they meant by feeling numb. What was happening to her? Suddenly she could faintly hear her favourite song, "I am comfortably numb...." by Pink Floyd in her head. When was it? She could hear the glasses clinking, her friends giggling... and that song... "Comfortably numb..." was she going crazy? Was she dead? Is this for real?

The hall was thunderous with applause. The fresh-faced group of young men and women threw their graduation hats high up in the air. Nalini screamed and cheered the loudest. All of 24 years and ready to go out in the world to carve her path as a computer engineer.

"Don't be satisfied with stories, how things have gone with others. Unfold your own myth."

– Rumi

The line summed up what she believed in and she had it immortalized below her smiling photograph in their graduation book.

Never one to follow rules. She was a tomboy, outspoken, impulsive and detested make-up, dresses and jewellery.

She hung out with the boys, wore baggy jeans, swore a lot, and drowned beer by the litre. She has been called many things in life. A tomboy, rebel child, twisted, in fact, her father once asked her mother with great worry if Nalini was a lesbian. She laughed it off when questioned by her mother, "What if I am Mom? Will you disown me? Seriously, both of you have never and will never understand me. Stop trying now!"

"Don't you dare do things that will spoil our name in society! As it is, we are having enough trouble dealing with questions about your late nights and alcoholic friends!" Her mother's warning fell on deaf ears as usual.

Sangamitra, her elder sister came to visit from Seattle in May with her year-old toddler. Mitra, as she was fondly called, was considered the epitome of feminine grace and beauty in the entire family and neighbourhood. Mitra was a darling especially of her paternal grandmother Kala as well their father Rama. Nalini grew up constantly compared to Mitra but eventually stopped resenting Mitra for it, as it was not her fault.

Nalini was eyeing a few international technology firms and had interviews scheduled with a few.

Sangamitra, an engineer herself, helped her sister prepare and in no time, she joined a firm and was well-settled at work. When a project came up in Seattle, Nalini wasted no time in proving her mettle and she started to pack her bags to fly to the Seattle office and spend time with her sister.

Seattle proved to be much more of a breather than the slightly stifling atmosphere at home.

During a long Saturday night out drinking with her office buddies, she struggled to walk up the stairs to her room, careful to not awaken her sister.

She changed with some difficulty into her night clothes. Her mobile beeped warning of low battery. She didn't care. She fell into her bed.

"Beep."

She turned to look at her laptop. She had a new mail in her inbox.

She caught her breath the moment she read the message.

Hey. I know it has been a long while. How is Seattle treating you? I am coming there for some work. Maybe we can catch up.

I know we had to leave things on a bitter note last we met.

I totally understand if you do not wish to meet me.

Ani

The floodgates of memories opened up once more.

1998. Uncle Raghu's wedding at Shornur, Kerala.

"Meet me at the terrace tonight once everyone is asleep."

It was a moonless night. The stars shone brighter in the village than she had ever seen in the Bangalore city skies.

She could make out his shadow in the far corner of the terrace. Her heartbeat rose with each step and grew louder and faster. The cool breeze did not calm her nerves. She had never before experienced anxiety, fear, excitement and a vague sense of happiness at the same time.

He turned and even under the faint light of the night sky, she could not help noticing how perfect that face was. His eyes crinkled at the edges when he smiled like that of an old man. It was very unlike any in their family, where almost everyone had doe-shaped large eyes. He never used a comb, or so it seemed. But every wavy lock knew exactly how to frame that magnificent face.

Aniruddha was the charming and offensive cousin that you have in almost every family. How one manages to mix both qualities is a marvel. The elders loved him one minute and hated him the very next. He would help Kala paati, into her chair and up the stairs and in the very next minute be found gambling in some corner with his notorious friends.

He was the star in the kids' circle and everyone wanted to follow him and take instructions from him in every game. At every wedding or family function, the children and teens would wait for the unusually tall Ani to walk in. Then the party would begin. With supreme confidence, a devil-may-care attitude, a penchant for mischief, and a mesmerizing mischievous grin, he was a magnet. Quite a contrast to his father Gopalan, who was a recluse. The teen girls and even some older women in the family could never have enough of Ani's attention.

As a teen, Nalini was awkward and gawky. Constant comparisons to Mitra throughout her childhood made her feel like the ugly duckling in the family. Dressing up like a tomboy, to look different from her sister did not help in stopping the incessant comparisons in school and family alike.

Nalini was a quiet child originally, unlike the rebel and boisterous young woman she turned into in her 20s.

She could not help but feel her glance slipping towards Ani during every family event. Each naughty smile and the way he turned his head ever so slightly to cause a lock of hair to fall away from his eye, "Sigh...!"

She was extra careful to never get caught. But today during the family photo shoot, she had not noticed him slyly and quietly walking behind her, and she stopped in her tracks as he whispered, "Meet me on the terrace tonight once everyone is asleep." He went away just as he appeared. Out of nowhere.

She stood at that same spot for what might have seemed an eternity to her. She could still feel his breath on her neck and ear as he whispered before vanishing into thin air. She felt her breath quicken, her eyes open wider, her cheeks blush and as she moved, there was a spring in every step.

It was now under the blissful night sky, that she felt her heart was going to crack open in her rib cage and fall out. She walked carefully as if some imaginary rustling leaves created a ruckus with each step of hers. She kept turning towards the door, dreading someone might come and see her. What a scandal that would be!

Their fathers were siblings. That made them first cousins. Gopalan avoided family functions altogether.

The First Cut

It took some years before his wife took charge of her own life and started to socialize within the family without waiting for her husband to accompany her. Nalini hence met Ani only when they were almost teenagers. She never felt that he was part of the family. He was this cool outsider who would walk in unannounced at functions and raise the energy levels in the room.

He motioned her to walk quickly towards him. In contrast to her present state, he seemed confident and patient. That made him even more attractive, in a dangerous manner. He fidgeted with his pockets and pulled out a small rectangular packet.

"Smoke?"

Nalini nodded in the negative vigorously.

Ani smirked. "Of what use is wearing baggy jeans and T-shirts when you have not even smoked once? How very disappointing!"

He smoked like one who has been doing it for a long time. She felt a cringe of jealousy seeing the way he held that cigarette so elegantly and delicately between his index and middle finger. The way the cigarette ever so slightly touched his lips.

He turned to look at her after a few puffs and she suddenly looked away embarrassed realizing she was unabashedly staring at him.

His hand reached out and he offered her the half-smoked cigarette.

She hesitated and took it, intending to feel his fingers touch against hers and placed it in her mouth, pursed her lips the way he did and sucked in the smoke. She quickly drew it out and suppressed a cough.

"Ha-ha... You will never understand what smoking is if you treat it like a poisonous gas!"

He snatched it from her and continued to caress the rest of the cigarette looking at the black void in front of him, completely ignoring her. He threw away the last bit and picked a second one, lit it with his lighter and smoked in silence, like nothing except him and the smoking roll of tobacco and paper existed in this universe.

She stood next to him, struggling not to fidget, feeling like a little fool. Why could she not have held the cigarette in a cooler manner? She should have taken a deep breath. He would have liked her better then.

A third cigarette. Nalini was now sure she had made a total fool of herself and tomorrow he will go back home and tell his college friends what a loser of a cousin he has.

Her limbs hurt from standing still. She did feel silly but just standing still without the slightest movement would redeem her of some pride, she felt.

"It will be dawn in a few hours," Ani spoke after what seemed an eternity.

The First Cut

Silence again. She shivered despite the fact it was not cold. She turned with great haste to go towards the door, still in doubt if the timing was right.

Out of nowhere, she saw him take a step slightly backwards, hold her left wrist, twist and pull her towards him and before she could balance herself better by placing her right foot on the ground, a pair of soft wet lips were on hers.

A fleeting moment later, she pulled back in bewilderment, breathless. She could taste the cigarette on her lips now. It felt like she had smoked the three cigarettes.

She looked at him with her fingers touching her lips, unsure of how to react. Ani just grinned and turned around to light up the next cigarette, and continued to look beyond the darkness. At that moment, it seemed Nalini's entire world had come to a standstill while nothing in Ani's had changed. His indifference had a hint of insensitivity that was too bothersome for her to analyse at this confusing turn of events.

She walked to the door and went to bed. Despite the fact, she would just be tossing and turning all night while her mind tried to fathom everything regarding tonight.

The next morning, Nalini and her parents had an early morning flight. As they stashed the luggage in the taxi, she kept turning her head to see if he would come to bid farewell. Disappointed she sat in the taxi and as it sped away threw a last glance. The car took a sharp right turn and a man was standing on the terrace watching the car. It was still time for the sun to rise. In the dim light, a faint red glow was seen moving in his right hand as he stylishly moved his hand to his mouth intermittently. She smiled. For she knew she was in love. For the first time.

There would be many more family functions and events where the young love blossomed, hidden away from the prying eyes of everyone, under their roof.

Rama and Vanaja found it surprising that their younger daughter who would be so hesitant about attending family functions, now suddenly was the first to come down with a packed suitcase. They assumed it was newfound love for the family. They were right!

Vanaja was delighted that her secondborn was dressing up like a girl now. At least for functions. She went overboard shopping for clothes, jewellery and make-up products for her daughter.

No one suspected a thing when they found that Aniruddha and Nalini had been calling each other very often. After all, they were first cousins. Brother and sister.

They would spend time in the evenings after the wedding/anniversary roaming the city markets/countryside, wherever they would gather for the family event.

The First Cut

It was a few years before the inevitable happened.

Gopalan's wife was a very inquisitive woman with a massive penchant for gossip. With some resistance from the family, he succeeded in marrying Rajitha, who he knew since his college days. The family had little choice but to support him as he had only recently recovered from depression after the untimely death of his first wife, Ani's mother, in a road traffic accident.

It was the 60th birthday of their granduncle, Kala's younger brother. A man born in dire poverty, it was his strong will, and intelligence combined with a convenient lack of ethics and morals in the world of business that made him a very successful industrialist and pulled the family into the high society circles from the small cottage they once struggled in.

By now Nalini was an engineering student and no longer an introvert. She had a gang of friends who had now introduced her to all the pubs and discos of Bangalore. She developed a great love for classic rock and discovered that the only way to completely understand Floyd, Bowie and Zeppelin was over many shots of tequila and Vodka.

The traditional phone calls over the landline were replaced with more discreet mobile phones and messages. Search as she may, she measured up every guy she met against Ani. And no one ever came close.

Ani had moved to Boston and was studying the History of Art. But that did not stop the messages or phone calls.

Sixtieth birthdays are considered very special amongst Hindus and call for a ceremonial traditional *pooja* (rites) and feast. Granduncle's sons had organized a party the next evening with dance and drinks to entertain the entire family who had come for the grand ceremony from the world over.

A video showing the family's beginnings, and early photographs brought tears to many eyes. The elders in the house were shown due respect and honoured.

Soon the party began as the elders went to rest their weary bones. The alcohol flowed, the music got louder and the party spilled into the courtyard and lawns.

The commotion that ensued, helped Ani and Nalini get away from the crowd. They had met after many months. While she was still in Bangalore, he had come from Boston for this function. And of course, because he knew she would be there too.

They walked along the other side of the venue, holding hands, catching up with each other's lives and realizing how much they missed each other. It started to rain. Ani had brought his car keys and they ran to the parking area to take shelter in the car. The cars were parked at right angles to the entrance of the main venue. In the absence of any light in that area, the two young lovers felt very secure.

The First Cut

Rajitha was bored with this fanciful family and was taking a walk on the terrace of the single-floored building. She was from a family that still struggled to make two ends meet and apart from her, no one had graduated from college. She could not but feel a tinge of jealousy from this overtly successful family that was celebrating the glory of three generations tonight. The constant comparisons with Jayam, Gopalan's much-loved deceased wife irked her. Ani never warmed up to her or welcomed her into his father's life. She was tired of measuring up to everything that was expected of her.

The rain was just a drizzle and she continued to pace. She moved to the opposite side of the terrace to get away from the din, caused by the music and merriment.

The skies warned of a huge downpour with lightning and thunder. In one flash of lightning, Rajitha thought she imagined someone in the empty car parking area. A second and third flash told her it was not an illusion. A gossip-monger all her life, she recognised a controversial story when she saw it. She knew at once who the two people walking hand-in-hand into the car were. She waited impatiently for the next flash of lightning. Within minutes, she saw the two young lovers kissing passionately. Rajitha knew this was the moment for her to shine and belittle this arrogant family that she found difficult to be a part of. She always felt she was looked down upon, which was the truth.

She ran downstairs to gather her husband, Nalini's parents and a few others in the family to the terrace in a panic-stricken voice. They ran up to the terrace in the rain with sombre worried faces, not knowing what to expect, always suspicious of Rajitha, certain that whatever it was, was not good news.

The next streak of lightning proved to be a very bright one; one that cast a spell of disappointment, shock and heartbreak and scandal on the entire family. What met their eyes froze them. Rama, the first to regain his composure, spoke in rage, "I am going to the parking lot now."

A few sobs broke the silence as the men went towards the door. Vanaja began to cry considering the sin her daughter committed.

Rajitha tried hard to not gloat and show the sadistic joy on her face. She bent down to comfort Vanaja who had slumped on the terrace floor not wanting to watch what was going on and what would happen next. To Rajitha's delight, her husband and Rama went down and banged the doors of the car, dragged the two youngsters and the fathers slapped their respective children, held them tight by the wrist and dragged them into the building.

After a long painful sleepless night, the elders in the house met the next morning to discuss the issue. The two youngsters were made to sit there and listen to the long speech from the elders. They kept their eyes fixed on the floor, tears welling up. All they could hear was a splatter of words, "Incest! What were you thinking?"; "Shame on our family! Never before..."; "Sinners! There is no place even in hell for you!"; "What sins have your parents committed to see this day? Karma, Karma...!" "Since when has this been going on? How did it begin?"; "How did we not see this coming? Rama, Gopal cannot you two manage your children?"

The only kind words came from Adhira and Mithila aunty. They tried in vain to restrain their siblings, asking them to be understanding and kind to the children.

After what seemed an endless interrogation, tears, and warnings, it was decided that the families take the two youngsters back to their homes and make sure they are not in touch. Granduncle came to meet Nalini's parents in their room and advised them to find her a suitable groom soon.

The next morning, the profound change in the faces of the two bright young lovers was evident. The youthful bright eyes and smile were replaced by a downcast look and dark circles under the eyes, downturned lips and sad faces.

The merriment had ended with two broken hearts that would take a long time to heal. Or, may never heal.

Ani went back to Boston and Nalini to her college and home in Bangalore. It would be a while before

Nalini began to smile again. In retaliation against her family for calling her names, she never thought they could, for an innocent love affair, she plunged herself into whisky and rum taking a step ahead of tequila and vodka. Her late nights grew longer, much to her parent's dismay.

The two lovers did not dare call each other. They were ridden with guilt at being called sinners. In their eyes, all they had experienced was innocent love. The allegations they were accused of were too shocking for them to bear even though they did realize this would be their reaction if they got caught. Nothing could prepare them for the insults and heartbreak their affair caused.

The ideal daughter, Mitra came to the rescue again by arriving home. She spent time with her sister. She had the maturity to deal with this matter delicately. Nalini slowly came back to her boisterous self after some months and began concentrating on her studies. Mitra promised to help her ace her exams and find a good placement.

After graduation, Mitra helped her choose a company with a strong foothold in the U.S. for the interview which would give her a chance to come there since she felt Nalini would emerge into a much healthier and emotionally strong person under her non-judgemental care instead of her parents.

Nalini had now been well-settled in her job and loved the environment of Seattle with the lake and

The First Cut

mountains. The scenic city did help to heal some ignored, long-forgotten wounds. Until now.

Her mind kept running over Ani's email. She spent the entire night recollecting the wonderful moments she had spent with him. The first time he spoke to her, that night the way the breeze played with his wavy locks while he smoked. The sudden memory of the fateful night their affair came into the open, made her shudder. Even after all these years. Bittersweet memories. She now knew what that meant.

She wondered for a long time. Four days later, she replied asking him to meet her at a small secluded cafe far away from her place of work and her sisters' as well.

She entered the cafe with great anxiety. She had taken care to apply an extra coating of lip colour and *kohl* that day. She resented that she did, but she could not bear to go without looking her best. After all, she was here to meet the first and only love of her life.

The tiny bells on the cafe door clinked and chimed as she entered. The yellow-themed lighting cast a beautiful sunset glow on the brown couches and tables and cream walls. She saw him. Distracted by a hundred memories of a time long gone, she walked slowly towards the table where he sat. He seemed leaner and the tan that he acquired under the Indian sun had faded. He kept his hair shorter now. He stood up when he saw her approach and smiled faintly. A smile that he felt would hide his pain. She looked more beautiful than ever. His wild rebellious tomboy lover had turned into a beautiful feminine swan.

"It is so good to finally see you. My, my how you have changed! Seattle seems to be treating you well, Nalini."

Nalini smiled, and blushed a little, despite herself. "Aniruddha, what brings you to Seattle?"

"Had an errand for my company. We are here to collect a few paintings for our art gallery and also to check out a new painter who has taken the art world by storm."

The coffee mugs arrived. The silence was palpable, a silence which years ago may have been filled by holding hands or a simple glance and smile.

A few sips of coffee later, Ani told her the news.

"I am getting engaged. Her name is Michelle. She works in my firm and is an Art major student. Her mom is South Indian, a Tam Bram (Tamil Brahmin) like us and her dad is American. But of course, she doesn't speak a word of Tamil!"

Nalini congratulated him and asked him when the engagement was to be.

"October. In Boston. Her family is settled there."

They spoke about their jobs, about how they find their lives here compared to back in India, and

The First Cut

exchanged family news. The coffee mugs were now empty. They stood up to bid farewell and wished each other luck in the years to come.

"I will send you the wedding invite. It will be the middle of next year in India mostly. Do try to make it."

They embraced and left the cafe.

Out in the humid air, as Nalini turned to leave, Ani screamed out,

"Nali! Boy, I wish I knew you would have turned out like this. I may have eloped with you that same night! Hahahaha..."

Nalini giggled and walked away. The smile on her face stayed for a long time.

As she neared her apartment, she admired herself on her composure and how well she took the news of his engagement. She was surprised by her maturity.

She slept blissfully that night.

The alarm clock wailed as usual at 6 am. She had forgotten to switch off the alarm last night as today was a Sunday. She angrily silenced it and went back to bed.

She was suddenly filled with an emptiness deep in her stomach. Her small apartment appeared to suffocate her. She found herself sobbing uncontrollably, like a child. It would be a while before she realized the reason. She opened up her laptop for the picture files.

Through the stream of tears, she painstakingly went through each album and deleted every photo in which Ani was present. She cried, even more, when she saw the photos of Uncle Raghu's wedding.

Once she was done, she wiped her tears, brewed a fresh cup of coffee, dressed up and went for a long walk. By the time she returned, it was noon and she felt much better.

It was time to move on, she decided.

She went to Mitra's house for lunch and told her she wanted to go back home to India.

In three weeks, Nalini was back on Indian soil, at home with her parents. She started with a new job and got together with her old friends. The only thing that had now changed was that she had grown quieter and refrained from alcohol.

In six months, Nalini's parents started to look for a suitable groom for her. Among the many proposals that came up, Nalini met a few guys and did not approve of them.

One day the parents of an engineer working in Texas showed up. Nalini's parents were very impressed with his educational credentials, salary and most importantly their horoscopes were a perfect match! The family was settled with their son in Austin. He was of average build, smart looking and well-behaved. Under enormous parental pressure, Nalini agreed to

The First Cut

marry Vinay. Since they were to leave for the U.S. in a month, the marriage was quickly arranged and fixed in the nearby temple in the presence of select relatives. Mitra was taken aback on hearing the urgency of the marriage. Mitra noticed that Nali looked miserable as a bride, but she could not help her.

Mitra and her family accompanied the bride back to Austin to her new home. Nalini had to quit her job since her company did not have offices in Austin. It was decided that she would look for a job once she settled in Austin. Mitra stayed in the groom's home for three days and then flew back home to Seattle.

Nalini had turned into a very quiet woman by now. She did not seem keen on getting to know her husband. She did not offer to help her mother-in-law unless asked to. They lived in a moderate-sized independent home with a small lawn. She would do what she was told with the housework, otherwise, she spent her days staring out of the first-floor window. She called her mother in India every three days, just to hear her voice and answered her in monosyllables.

"Nali, are you well? Are you having a good time?"

"Yes"

"Are you eating properly? Why don't you tell them to find some help with the housework?"

"Okay"

"I miss you, kanna. I hope everything is okay. It takes time to adjust in any marriage. Don't you worry."

"All right"

"Your father and I pray for your well-being every day. I will call you soon. Take care, my child."

Nalini would place down the phone and wipe away the silent tears on her face every time.

The phone calls grew longer and longer apart. Her parents were worried.

Many times, Nalini's mother-in-law would pick up the phone and speak courteously. But on asking about Nalini, she would come up with vague reasons.

"She has gone to the market."

"She is asleep."

"She is in the neighbour's house."

It was eight months since the wedding. It had been three full months since they heard her voice. One day, the phone rang and Nalini's mother picked it up.

"Amma!" Nalini wailed

"Nali, what is the matter dear?"

"Amma!" She was sobbing uncontrollably and gasping for breath each time.

"They.... *(sob)*...They lock me. No food. He hit me. *(sob) (sob)*"

"Nali, calm down my child, tell me again, what is happening? I was so worried. I asked Mitra to come down to Austin. She is busy... You did not call for three months!"

"Vinay started to hit me Ma... I threatened them with police action. His mom hit me too. They have kept me locked in a room. No food. I escaped through the window. I am speaking from a public phone. Amma, help me..." Nalini managed to speak through multiple gasps for breath.

"Nali, you go straight to the police. I am coming there with your father."

The phone went dead.

Nalini cried and screamed in the phone booth. The kind man waiting outside the booth who gave this heavily injured and bleeding woman money to make the phone call called the police and ambulance. By the time the ambulance got there, Nalini had fainted and lay in a pool of her blood in the cramped booth.

Nalini went in and out of consciousness. She could hear her sister's voice in between. She was sedated. The doctors found no major damage in the computed tomography scans of her head. Her hair was shaved off and the extensive scalp tear was sutured. The multiple facial, hand and head abrasions, bruises and cuts were addressed and dressed. When she was fully conscious, she found Mitra holding her hand and speaking softly to her.

"How are you, my baby?"

Nalini nodded. Mitra's eyes were swollen and red and fresh tears poured yet again.

"Mom and Dad will arrive tomorrow. I have informed the airlines to send a message to them in flight that you are okay."

Nalini went back to sleep.

She was safe now.

Nalini was discharged a week later after a few sessions with a counsellor specialising in dealing with victims of domestic abuse.

She learned that a case had been filed by her family with the police against Vinay and his mother.

Nalini told her family she needed to go home to Bangalore and leave all this behind. She would pursue the case after she recovered emotionally.

The cool Bangalore air welcomed her as the flight door opened. She felt as if she were always home and that the immediate past was just a nightmare.

She spent all day at home looking out of the window. Every morning she looked at her reflection in the mirror and another woman with a shaved head and multiple scars and bruises on her face and head looked back at her. Her eyes conveyed profound sadness and hopelessness. She walked around the house from room to room like a ghost.

The First Cut

It had been four months since she came home. She was still not ready to go back for the trial.

Her hair was growing again. Her bruises had healed. But it would be a long time before she was herself again.

Mitra had booked her tickets to Ladakh for the next month. She was certain a trip would do her good.

One mundane afternoon, she was looking at the neighbourhood children playing cricket on the streets. Her mother was on the phone and sounded very anxious.

"Poor Gopalan! Ani broke his engagement again. This is the second time in two years. His only son. How will he not be worried..."

She gave Nalini a cup of coffee and turned on the radio.

Nalini sipped the coffee and fixed her eyes on the game of cricket outside the window.

The radio softly played in the background...

"The first cut is the deepest, baby I know

The first cut is the deepest

But when it comes to bein' lucky, he's cursed

When it comes to lovin' me, he's worst...

I still want you by my side

Just to help me dry the tears that I've cried..."

THE UNINVITED GUESTS

What did you eat for lunch yesterday?

Some of you may have zero recollection of the same.

Have you ever wondered, truly wondered about the food you eat? Is not this food assimilated into your body at the cellular level helping you create, preserve and heal your own? Does not this food become part of you?

Imagine if every morsel you have eaten in life forever remains a part of your being and has a memory of the same.

You had a mango when you were five years old. You threw the seed away in an open ground while playing. This mango tree has produced fruit and fed birds, humans, monkeys, squirrels and many more. Some of the fruits have entered Mother Earth again and given birth to new trees. Do you wonder if all those who eat the fruits of the same tree are connected in some way? Does this establish a connection between the tree and those it fed? If so, how deep would the connection go? Will it remain across time and landscapes?

You would not have time for such nonsensical utterances of mine.

Forgive me for my senile ruminations.

★ ★ ★

"There, there! How handsome my boys look!"

Kala beamed at Raghu and Rama. The neatly pressed clean white shirts, dark blue pants, and well-oiled combed hair impressed their mother. She was used to seeing them covered in dirt and grime most of the time.

"Before I forget," Kala rushed to the kitchen bringing back a steel container and handed it to Rama.

"I made some jackfruit *payasam* (pudding) for Sukku. Carry it carefully."

It was Sukanya's tenth birthday and the celebrations were to be grand.

Ramakrishnan and Raghuvaran – Rama and Raghu as they were called, walked happily to the bus stop and were soon en route to their eldest sister Kamakshi's house near the city centre. The ride was around 25 minutes and they were eager to meet their niece.

Sukanya, Rama and Raghu were more like cousins than niece and uncles. Sukanya was a few years older than Raghu and a year younger than Rama.

She was the first grandchild and the apple of her grandfather's eye.

The bus conductor smiled widely at the two boys. He knew the family well.

"You look so good! Where are you off to children?"

They happily told him their destination.

"Oh, how lovely! Did your Amma pack sweets for Sukanya?"

They got down at the bus stop closest to their sister's house, and walked 10 minutes to reach the house.

The tall, wide wooden gates were ajar. The boys pushed it open to see the cream walls of the palatial house with a red-sloping tiled roof.

They walked along the tiled pathway up to the verandah.

The front door was wide open and many guests were darting to and fro. The boys were excited to meet their niece but a little uncomfortable seeing the crowd of people within.

They took off their slippers in the courtyard and stepped into the verandah. They hesitated, feeling a tad shy and lingered here for a few minutes, waiting to catch a familiar face at the door. Some guests came in and walked past them inside the house.

Kamakshi walked outside to receive some guests and came upon her young brothers. She didn't say a word and walked with the guests from the gate into the living room and returned hastily to the boys.

"Come here, don't stand there. Come!"

She directed them to the backyard and confronted the boys.

"Who called you here? Who invited you?"

Rama looked at her in confusion and was hurt by the accusatory tone in her voice. Raghu was too young to appreciate the nuances of her tone. He had always been afraid of his eldest sister. She had an arrogant and authoritative demeanour.

"Akka, Sukku's birthday. Amma sent payasam."

Rama replied meekly.

Kamakshi snatched the vessel from Raghu's hands and walked a few steps and put it down near the well. The steel vessel clanged against the black rock it now sat on. With that sound, the morale of the boys was further lowered.

"I did not invite any of you! How dare you come?"

Rama and Raghu looked at each other in hurt and confusion.

"I have Sukku's friends, their parents and my in-laws inside. We have important people inside. I cannot let beggars like you in and wreck the party. Off you go back to that beggar woman who birthed you."

Rama stared her dead in the eye. No one speaks ill of his Amma.

He regained confidence in his voice as his rage rose.

"SHE IS YOUR MOTHER TOO!"

Kamakshi baulked for a few seconds at this unexpected outburst from the young lad.

"You may hate her but she is my mother and Raghu's mother."

Kamakshi regained her footing and dominance and took a step towards her brothers.

"We don't need anything from her and I want you begone before anybody sees you."

The boys turned around and started to walk towards the gate.

Rama held Raghu's hands tight and noticed Raghu wiping his tears.

Rama took deep breaths and counted in his mind. He would not cry. He was not a child anymore. He tried to convince himself that he was strong. He would not give his evil sister the satisfaction of seeing his tears.

He then remembered and let go of Raghu's hand and ran past Kamakshi towards the well.

"Where...? How dare..."

She stopped her questions as she saw Rama pick up the payasam container.

Rama joined his brother and continued ahead.

They could hear Kamakshi's heavy footsteps behind them. She followed them to the gate and the moment they stepped out; she closed the gates and latched it from within.

The children crossed the road and started to walk towards the bus stop. Raghu's tears had dried. But the floodgates had just opened for his sensitive elder brother. The tears streamed down his face, but Rama did not move his hands anywhere close to his face.

The bus ride back home was in complete silence. It was dusk by the time they reached home. The grey skies added to the cloud of gloom on the children's heads.

They entered the house and Kala came to the living room from the kitchen.

"So, did you get to play with Sukku?"

The grim tear-stained faces and the full vessel of payasam in their hands revealed the entire happenings to Kala.

Kala silently took the vessel to the kitchen.

"Go and have a bath. I will set the table for dinner."

She went to the kitchen and fried a few extra poppadums for the boys as a treat.

As the hot oil simmered and spluttered, buffing up the flat dough cakes, Kala allowed herself the luxury of expressing emotions in the safety of her kitchen.

Like her son Rama, she didn't bring up her hand even once to wipe her eyes.

She whispered, "She will pay. She will pay for hurting my innocent boys. Devi, my mother! You will ensure she pays dearly for this pain."

★ ★ ★

The afternoon gust of strong breeze never fails to come at this time during June. It is nearing that time again. The fag end of what they call 'mango season'. I long for the rain. I find life is undisturbed during the rains. It is the time to sprout new leaves and heal broken branches and wounds. It will be time for peace, to contemplate, to relook at what to create, and how to grow.

But I feel a little pain this particular day. It was on this day years ago, that two little children who grew up eating the flesh of my fruits, passed by me with tears streaming down their faces, ignoring the breeze that brought down a fresh batch of my children: the mangoes to the ground.

What were we talking about earlier? I forget at my age.

Oh yes, have you ever wondered, if you stay connected to the mother source of every food that you have ever eaten?

13 DAYS

It was warm and wet, sunshine and rain, clear skies and clouds, laughter and tears, old and young, past and present. It was a day that bore heavily on the minds of those gathered in the house. An emotional upheaval in all the lives under this roof.

"Sunshine through pouring rains is a sign of good luck. Something good is around the corner."

Adhira interrupted Chitra's thoughts, joining her on the steps of the verandah.

"Amma would say that. When I was heading to school to collect my tenth standard board exam results, it rained just like today with bright sunshine. I was confident that I would have passed the exam and thankfully I did!"

Chitra smiled at her favourite aunt. "Do you know my Amma told me the same thing when I went to see the college admission list and the weather was the same?"

Mithila and Sharada entered the living room with steel glass tumblers and a huge vessel filled with piping hot filter coffee. Soon the living room was brimming with the entire family.

"Have you children heard about the baby elephant our uncle Anjaneyu had?"

All the youngsters turned towards Uncle Gopalan.

"Anjaneyu was Amma's eldest brother. A filthy rich man who made his money by building some of the first factories in the city and state. He purchased a baby elephant so his children could have a pet! Imagine how huge his house and courtyard may have been!"

Adhira interrupted, "Amma used to send me to get milk from their house. I remember standing at the gate and watching our cousins play with the elephant. I think they named him Keshavan. Such a sweet little thing that baby was!"

"Did not you guys play with Keshavan? I mean how many people can claim to have grown up playing with a baby elephant, right? Crazy!" Aniruddha smiled imagining the possibility.

Adhira exchanged glances with Gopalan and Mithila.

"Have you forgotten that we were children of poor parents? None of our rich cousins wanted us around them. I used to hate going to their house. Waiting like a maid's daughter at the gate or back entrance for a litre of milk. I hated it but who dare refuse Amma?"

Mithila responded, "After you, I was next in line to beg for that litre of milk at their place. I used to feel so embarrassed standing at their back gate. This was my uncle's home for God's sake! Yet the way they treated us when Amma did so much for them all her life! Those bastard cousins of ours, one day let their dog chase me. I was barely five years old. That dog chased me for quite a few minutes when they kept laughing. Scared me out of my wits. Took me the longest time to get over my fear of dogs."

Mithila paused to compose her anger and pain.

"How sadistic! And to do that to a child! Amma saw me crying that day. I had fallen and scraped my arms and knees. The milk in my hand had spilt all over my clothes. She never sent anyone to uncle's house again."

The mood turned sombre. They were hearing this episode for the first time. Rama, Gopalan and Sharada turned red in the face with rage. How could they commit such cruelty on their youngest sister?

A car honked in the narrow lane. Ani rushed out to open the gates to let the vehicle in. Raghu and his daughters arrived.

Raghu had brought breakfast for everybody. The kitchen table had a beautiful spread of puttu kadala curry, *idli, medu vada, dosa, aapam, sevai* and more. Chitra headed out immediately after breakfast with Raghu's daughters as promised, to explore the neighbourhood and local market.

Mukundan came down from the terrace with his flute.

"*Enna da*? Done with practice? Come sit with us. When will we meet like this again?"

Mukundan sat next to his uncle Raghu.

"Mumbai is suiting you well. Adhira, your son has grown fitter and more handsome!"

Ani walked up to his cousin and playfully hit him on the head.

"I have grown fitter but Ani, you have become broader *da* in the U.S.!"

Ani held Mukundan in a tight embrace and tossed his curly locks and laughed.

The cooks arrived with the prepared lunch feast.

Banana leaves were laid out on the floor of the spacious living room, with mats for seating on the side. They were expecting around 35 guests for lunch – friends and people from the neighbourhood.

As they laid out the leaves, Sharada spoke, "I forgot for a few moments that I am placing these leaves for the final thirteenth-day lunch of Amma's death rites. Feels unreal, doesn't it?"

"It does. I keep expecting her to come up behind me in her precious kitchen to scold me for not doing things the way she would."

Adhira listened to her sisters' exchanges as she arranged the vessels, trying in vain to stop her tears.

The guests walked in over the next two hours, ate lunch, and left conveying their condolences and prayers for Kala. Kala was extremely loved, respected and feared.

There was not a single neighbour who was not grieving. The men and women seemed as broken as the children who lost their beloved mother.

Chitra returned with the girls.

Ani ran up to her at the gates.

"Chitralekha! Doctor *ayacha* (Have you finally become a doctor)?"

"*Po da* (Get lost)! It has been years since I became one. Now I will be an Ophthalmologist in another year."

"I know da. Am teasing you *chumma* (just like that)."

Chitra never did like Ani and did her best to keep her distance. A very damaging personality – in her words – to others and his own self.

Ani lowered his voice to a whisper as they walked towards the main house entrance.

"Chitra, is not Nali coming? How is she, where is she?"

"*Idu tevai ya* (Is this necessary)? Have you not faced enough Ani? So has she. Let go. She has been through hell!"

"I know, I know! I am worried sick. Please kanna, please please just tell me if she is okay."

Chitra glared at him for a few seconds. The concern he showed seemed genuine.

"She is going for counselling sessions. She went on a trip to Ladakh recently. She is amazingly better since the trip. I overheard Amma talking to Vanaja aunty. I think Nalini is moving back to the U.S. for work in a few months."

Ani appeared relieved and strangely happy to hear that.

Chitra read his mind, "No. Absolutely no Ani! I will not bother that you are my elder brother. I will come and whack your head if you contact or meet her. Let her be. Please! Be kind. Be sensible. Let her heal and live in peace at least now!"

Ani bowed his head low and nodded.

Chitra found it hard to trust him though. Ani was as unpredictable as the seas.

Now the entire family sat together for lunch taking turns to serve each other.

"Why have not Sukku, Amu, Murthy and others come?"

"Mitra is expecting a baby very soon; regarding Nalini, you know. She needs time, and to be on her own. Sukku is on her way with Vanya. Murthy is taking care of the children as his wife is travelling," answered Sharada.

"And Amu? I have not seen her in 15 years. Most of us have not seen her since she moved abroad,"

"Gopal anna, Amritha is not well. They have found a lump and they are busy having it tested, Until they know for sure, it is worrying."

"Oh, the poor child! Don't you worry. She is young. Won't be the thing to lose sleep over. Mark my words."

Rama stood up to walk up to the new arrivals. Sukanya and Vanya entered. Mukundan was elated to see that Vanya had brought along her violin, just as he had requested her to. Though Vanya was his niece, he was younger than her by some years.

"Sukku *ma*, epudi irrukai (how are you dear)? Vanya, I couldn't recognise you with this short hair."

Sukanya hugged Sharada, who was the closest to her late mother and her favourite aunt as well. Sukanya was not close to most on this side of the family, unlike her father's side. She often wondered why her mother so intensely disliked her siblings, and why the siblings also chose to maintain distance from Kamakshi. But the siblings never had the heart to tell her the truth about her mother's misdeeds. Sukanya herself was often blind to those.

"Is it not better to believe that one's mother is a good woman and human being than otherwise?" was the reasoning the elder siblings gave.

'Selective memory and interpretation', to quote Mithila's words was the widely held opinion though concerning Sukanya. The relationship between Kala's younger children and Sukanya was like that between cousins, rather than aunt/uncle-niece. Sukanya, Adhira, Mithila, and Rama played together as children within a decade of each other.

Rama suspected that Kamakshi suffered from certain psychiatric disorders. Else pathological lying, massive alteration in moods and behaviours, lack of empathy, a tendency for cruelty, deep jealousy and insecurities could not be explained. Fortunately, the daughter and granddaughter did not inherit these disorders.

Post lunchtime, everyone continued to sit in the living room enjoying hearing the birds chirping and witnessing sunshine in the thriving courtyard.

"I wish we were all together here for a wedding and that Amma could have seen us all under the same roof. Does anyone remember when we last met like this?"

"Appa's death rites, Adhira. Ten years ago," came the answer from the inner bedroom. Murali walked out of his hibernation in his mother's room to join his young siblings.

Raghu got up to make room to seat their eldest brother. Murali, the quietest in the family had chosen to remain unmarried and gave his mother company till her last breath. He and Kala were the only inhabitants of the house for the last few decades.

Murali rarely spoke. His siblings suspected he was showing signs of early dementia.

He randomly started reminiscing about an incident of the past.

"Sharada, do you remember our uncle Anjaneyu? Back in the day, we used to stay in Muvattupuzha. Uncle had come to visit Amma. Anjaneyu was the oldest brother among the three brothers Amma had. When he entered the house, he saw Amma sitting at the entrance late afternoon, eating rice with a piece of green chilli. Our grandmother was a very cruel woman. Amma would hardly have anything to eat once all had their meals, meals that were cooked by her.

Uncle was so pained to see this. He left without a word. The next day the courtyard was filled with grains and vegetables of every kind. Uncle had returned with produce that filled up two bullock carts. Grandma and the entire family went out to see him unload everything. Amma was very emotional. Uncle ran his hand over Amma's head as she cried. He walked up to our grandmother and told her, 'Take care of her. She is our younger sister. Ensure she gets good food twice a day at the very least.'

Amma told me years later, she saw him wipe his eyes, as he left in haste."

The younger children had heard this episode in their mother's life for the first time. They knew Kala was tortured by the in-laws, but hearing how hungry she was in that period, as a young hardworking mother, was heartbreaking.

Vanya and Mukundan readied their instruments, happy to have their Uncle Murali as well in the room. Right on time, a young beautiful girl with long wavy black hair walked into the house.

Mithila beamed as her youngest entered. Lakshmi had completed a college project the day before and had taken the first flight out to Kochi.

Lakshmi greeted everyone and joined the musicians.

It was a beautiful concert: Vanya played the violin with her western classical background; Mukundan played the flute, with his Hindustani music background and Lakshmi who was trained in Carnatic music was the vocalist. They played and sang for close to an hour and ended to much applause.

Adhira shed tears throughout the programme, applauding the most.

She choked up as she said, "Lakshmi, you have Amma's voice, my dear!"

Chitra commented, "Those zoom practice sessions worked guys! Great performance! And here I was thinking that you must be gossiping the entire time."

Everyone laughed.

"Paati would have been so proud to have seen this." Chitra hugged Lakshmi.

"Did you know Mithila, when Appa was in the movie industry, a director friend had come home. Amma was singing a lullaby to put Rama to sleep. He heard her sing and asked her to sing in a movie."

This excited the children, and all ears and eyes were on Murali.

"But Appa, knowing how rotten the industry was especially in those days, flatly refused and asked the director to get out of the house!"

Shiva was known to be over-protective of the women folk in the house.

"Tell us more stories from those days, *Mama* (uncle)" Lakshmi requested.

Sharada got everyone coffee.

The sun was still bright up in the sky.

"You loved your paati. But did you know she was feared by many? Isn't it Gopal?"

Gopal nodded his head, "Amma was such a powerful figure. Even I was afraid of her. Even today despite the fact she is no more. So is Sharada. The things we have witnessed...I would have found it hard to believe if I had just heard it, instead of seeing it."

"Enough Gopal and Murali. The children don't need to know more."

"No, no. Tell us! We will love paati always, no matter what. You know that!"

Gopal glanced at Adhira and Mithila who looked helpless.

"When Amma was thrown out of our previous home, she was pregnant with our youngest. She went into preterm labour and we lost that child. Amma survived that ordeal and blood loss luckily. The very next day, we heard the money lender who threw us out had died. He had fallen down the stairs."

There was an eerie silence as he continued.

"For the next ten years, we kept moving houses. There was one landlord, Keshavan Nair who misbehaved with Amma. Amma left that house the same evening. The next day, one of Amma's friends came running to the house and looked very shaken. She held a hand to her chest and asked 'Kala, what have you done? Who did you pray to? Keshavan died last night!'

What scared me that day, was Amma's face on hearing this. She looked calm and collected as if she was expecting this. Amma folded her hands and thanked the Goddess. 'You listen to me as always Devi.'

I alone can give you six more such events, Sharada and Murali some more.

Amma was no ordinary woman, I always knew."

Chitra was a sceptic, but Mithila noticed she seemed to look a little shocked hearing this.

Sukanya broke her silence. "Amma told me this about paati. I had trouble having a child. Paati had prayed for me at the Devi temple and told me that I would have a daughter in less than a year. It gives me goosebumps how right she was!"

"Amma had a remarkable memory. She remembered every single person's birthday and performed puja at the temple without fail." Mithila recollected.

"They had a horrible relationship, Amma and Appa, didn't they? Yet they had so many children. Ha ha. Appa was another interesting character. He lived so many lives in a single one!"

"Very true Rama, Appa is another book altogether. A fascinating man, though a conflicted husband and father," added Gopalan.

Raghu looked sad. "I feel my children missed out on much of our parents."

"They have us as grandparents Raghu!" Adhira hugged her youngest nieces.

Sharada and Murali brought something from the kitchen. They handed a small jar to each sibling. "This is the last batch of mango pickle Amma made."

It was a moment of hard reality and tears flowed.

Everyone would leave today and the next day Murali would be alone in the house.

This evening and night were special. The past and present merged like ink in water. Timelines were blurred. The family bonded like never before.

Sukanya bid farewell and left with Vanya.

Murali retired to his room to sleep.

Rama broached the much-dreaded topic.

"Regarding the house. I do think we might need to sell it, as none of us would be staying here. And this is what some of you want. But I feel it is only right if we could wait and let Murali anna live here for the rest of his life, with dignity. He looked after Amma and Appa in their old age when we were busy with our lives."

Everyone agreed wholeheartedly and was relieved that the house would exist and welcome them for some more years.

"That day. I was a child but Amma's tears, I can never forget. When we had to leave our old house. The way she ran for miles and miles! Nobody helped her. The tears she later shed for the baby that died…" Mithila broke down and cried her heart out.

Adhira walked to her and held her by the shoulders. "It is a great decision, Rama and Gopal. This is the house that gave Amma security and dignity after years of rental rooms. It was me, Rama, and Mithila who saw this house being built brick by brick. We are more attached to this house than you can imagine. Losing Appa, then Amma. To add to that losing this house, would break us all. Thank you for this. Thank you."

The silence that followed filled everyone with peace and calm.

The siblings had not been able to sleep well for the past 12 days. But tonight they slept soundly. It seemed that Kala's soul may have finally found peace and moved to another realm.

The next day many farewells were exchanged and the number of inhabitants in the house kept decreasing by the hour.

Adhira and Mithila asked Murali to visit them often, despite knowing he would not do that. Murali never left Ernakulam. He lived in Mumbai for a few years in his younger days and hated it.

Raghu who stayed nearby promised to keep an eye on Murali.

Mithila handed the bags to the driver. Chitra and Lakshmi were seated in the car.

"Check if you have the tickets, Chitra!"

"Yes Amma, come soon. We are already late."

Mithila walked out of the gates and opened the car door. She glanced at the entrance of the house, out of habit since childhood. The same scene for so many years, so many visits before this, the one stable thing in life, that pillar in her life, the one who gave her life…would always be standing there as Mithila left the house..to go to school, college, after her wedding, returning after vacations…

This time though there was no one there.

MEANDERINGS IN THE MEADOW

As I sit on the meadow watching the white cloud,
I let go of prejudices that make my mind cloud.

The cacophony of humans, irate serves to drive,

I left the city, resolved to maintain my drive.

The birds swinging by the blue skies over my head,

Oh, freedom, sweet freedom is where I need to head.

My shoelaces lay untied, dusty and worn out,

While my feet ache to escape their confines to burst out.

Not a sound I hear in this mountainous silence,

Yet my inner thoughts and dilemmas I struggle to silence.

Time is of the essence, and one day I will be mature.

Until then let me lie in my bliss here with this wine so mature.

ACKNOWLEDGEMENTS

The foundation of my writing and storytelling was laid down in infancy. My parents and grandparents are brilliant storytellers and these stories formed the very core of my young imagination. Hence, I have my family to be grateful to, for allowing the vivid imagery of that child to grow and never attempting to restrain it. The Krishna and Spiderman stories concocted by my mother (Geetha) to make me eat, the princess stories that my father (Rajan) read to me after a tiring day at work, Grandpa's library with Ramayana, Mahabharata, Amar Chitra Katha, Classics Illustrated, Austens, Brontes, Dickens', and countless other treasures that I grew up with, birthed the writer in me long before the surgeon. I had my struggles with grammar rules and my sister, Anjana, who studied English literature was always there to provide an expert opinion. She is my urban dictionary and ensures I keep up with the changing times. Anjana, a self taught illustrator has designed the cover page of this book using various elements from the stories.

My love for English as a language is also thanks to my English language teachers, my aunt Shyama who is a very talented writer and a voracious reader.

Acknowledgements

I had some wonderful people who walked into my life and helped the writer in me blossom. Patricia Chandrashekar's home and creative writing sessions was the first place I tapped my skills and allowed myself to be vulnerable as a writer. Anamika Kundu had my words in print for the first time in her anthology. The story was titled *Wine* in the anthology *Changed Forever*. Anamika ma'am gave me the confidence to go ahead and publish my collection of stories instead of waiting for a few more decades. She edited this book for me, long before I even approached a publishing company. She called me periodically to keep track of my work and pushed me through the phases where I neglected my writing/editing work. She would pick up my phone day and night, and I would call her only when I had these 'Aha' moments. My book was done but I didn't have a final title for quite a while. My favourite call to her was one late night in November when I woke her up to tell her I finally had a title for my book. She loved the title (the very title printed on the cover) and how she celebrated that moment with me!

Pankaj Pradhan, my brilliant friend! I treasure every email feedback I received from him regarding my stories. Ujwal Mantha, for that one fateful phone call in November past midnight, that shaped the book into this current version. Jerry Everard, my dear friend from the violin circle, for providing me with such thoughtful input on the stories.

Acknowledgements

My Poppins, Zoya, Bagheera, Sher Khan, Fiona, Tommy, Fawn, Nora, Lisa, Rudolf, Momo Chan, Midori, Cat-rina and Marvel provide me great joy in life and have been my teachers in mindfulness. I am a better writer and am more creative due to them. I finished writing this book on November 8 in Kashi and the last line I typed was the dedication page for Tommy. On the evening of the 9th, my beloved cat Tommy died after bravely battling ill health for three months. When I reached home on the 10th, I laid flowers on Tommy's grave in our courtyard. I learned so much about life from this little cat, and not a day goes by when as a family we don't miss him.

I thank my capable team at Notion Press for enabling me to achieve this dream and helping in bringing this book to light.

I thank my family, teachers, friends, and well-wishers wholeheartedly. I especially wish to extend my gratitude to my online readers. The feedback you have shared with me on public forums or in private conversations left an indelible impression on me and proved to be the force that pushed this book through all the processes it did to reach here in print.

Writing this book has been a cathartic process for me. I trust that you, my beloved reader felt some of that as well.

Anuradha

ABOUT THE AUTHOR

Anuradha has always loved writing. The writing of these stories has covered more than a decade to finally come alive in this book. Anuradha plays the violin and piano. She loves travelling, trekking and exploring and often pens down her experiences. She lives in a large family comprising her parents, sister, two dogs and a dozen cats. Anuradha is an Ophthalmic Plastic Surgeon by profession. This is her first book.